PENGUIN TWENTIETH-CENTURY CLASSICS

LOSER TAKES ALL

Graham Greene was born in 1904. On coming down from Balliol College, Oxford, he worked for four years as a sub-editor on *The Times*. He established his reputation with his fourth novel, *Stamboul Train*. In 1935 he made a journey across Liberia, described in *Journey Without Maps*, and on his return was appointed film critic of the *Spectator*. In 1926 he had been received into the Roman Catholic Church and visited Mexico in 1938 to report on the religious persecution there. As a result he wrote *The Lawless Roads* and, later, his famous novel *The Power and the Glory*. *Brighton Rock* was published in 1938 and in 1940 he became literary editor of the *Spectator*. The next year he undertook work for the Foreign Office and was stationed in Sierra Leone from 1941 to 1943. This later produced his novel, *The Heart of the Matter*, set in West Africa.

As well as his many novels, Graham Greene wrote several collections of short stories, four travel books, six plays, three books of autobiography – *A Sort of Life*, *Ways of Escape* and *A World of My Own* (published posthumously) – two of biography, and four books for children. He also contributed hundreds of essays, and film and book reviews, some of which appear in *Reflections*. Many of his novels and short stories have been filmed, and *The Third Man* was written as a film treatment. A great number of his film writings, reviews, scripts and interviews have been published as *Mornings in the Dark: A Graham Greene Film Reader* (1993). Graham Greene was a member of the Order of Merit and a Companion of Honour.

Graham Greene died in April 1991. Among the many people who paid tribute to him on his death were Kingsley Amis: 'He will be missed all over the world. Until today, he was our greatest living novelist'; Alec Guinness: 'He was a great writer who spoke brilliantly to a whole generation. He was almost prophet-like with a surprising humility'; and William Golding: 'Graham Greene was in a class by himself . . . He will be read and remembered as the ultimate chronicler of twentieth-century man's consciousness and anxiety.'

WORKS BY GRAHAM GREENE

NOVELS

The Man Within   Stamboul Train   It's a Battlefield
England Made Me   A Gun for Sale   Brighton Rock
The Confidential Agent   The Power and the Glory
The Ministry of Fear   The Heart of the Matter
The Third Man   The Fallen Idol   The End of the Affair
Loser Takes All   The Quiet American   Our Man in Havana
A Burnt-Out Case   The Comedians   Travels with My Aunt
The Honorary Consul   The Human Factor
Doctor Fischer of Geneva or The Bomb Party
Monsignor Quixote   The Tenth Man
The Captain and the Enemy

SHORT STORIES

Collected Short Stories (*including* Twenty-One Stories,
A Sense of Reality *and* May We Borrow Your Husband?)
The Last Word and other stories

TRAVEL

Journey Without Maps   The Lawless Roads
In Search of a Character   Getting to Know the General

ESSAYS

Collected Essays   Yours etc.   Reflections

PLAYS

The Living Room   The Potting Shed   The Complaisant Lover
Carving a Statue   The Return of A. J. Raffles   The Great Jowett
Yes and No   For Whom the Bell Chimes

AUTOBIOGRAPHY

A Sort of Life   Ways of Escape
Fragments of Autobiography   A World of My Own

BIOGRAPHY

Lord Rochester's Monkey   An Impossible Woman

CHILDREN'S BOOKS

The Little Train   The Little Horse-Bus
The Little Steamroller   The Little Fire Engine

GRAHAM GREENE

LOSER TAKES ALL

PENGUIN BOOKS

in association with William Heinemann Ltd

PENGUIN BOOKS
An imprint of Penguin Random House LLC
375 Hudson Street
New York, New York 10014
penguin.com

First published in Great Britain by William Heinemann Ltd 1955
First published in the United States of America in a Viking Compass Edition
by The Viking Press 1958
Published in Penguin Books in Great Britain 1971
Reset and reprinted from the Collected Edition 1977
Published in Penguin Books in the United States of America 1977

A serial version of this book appeared in
the United States of America in
Harper's Magazine

ISBN 978-0-14-018542-3

Printed in the United States of America

11 10 9 8 7

Set in Linotype Times

Dear Frere,

As we have been associated in business and friendship for a quarter of a century I am dedicating this frivolity without permission to you. Unlike some of my Catholic critics, you, I know, when reading this little story, will not mistake me for 'I', nor do I need to explain to you that this tale has not been written for the purposes of encouraging adultery, the use of pyjama tops, or registry office marriages. Nor is it meant to discourage gambling.

Affectionately and gratefully,

Graham Greene

PART ONE

1

I SUPPOSE the small greenish statue of a man in a wig on a horse is one of the famous statues of the world. I said to Cary, 'Do you see how shiny the right knee is? It's been touched so often for luck, like St Peter's foot in Rome.'

She rubbed the knee carefully and tenderly as though she were polishing it. 'Are you superstitious?' I said.

'Yes.'

'I'm not.'

'I'm so superstitious I never walk under ladders. I throw salt over my right shoulder. I try not to tread on the cracks in pavements. Darling, you're marrying the most superstitious woman in the world. Lots of people aren't happy. We are. I'm not going to risk a thing.'

'You've rubbed that knee so much, we ought to have plenty of luck at the tables.'

'I wasn't asking for luck at the tables,' she said.

2

THAT night I thought that our luck had begun in London two weeks before. We were to be married at St Luke's Church, Maida Hill, and we were going to Bournemouth for the honeymoon. Not, on the face of it, an exhilarating programme, but I thought I didn't care a damn where we went so long as Cary was there. Le Touquet was within our means, but we thought we could be more alone in Bournemouth – the Ramages and the Truefitts were going to Le Touquet. 'Besides, you'd lose all our money at the Casino,' Cary said, 'and we'd have to come home.'

'I know too much about figures. I live with them all day.'

'You won't be bored at Bournemouth?'

'No. I won't be bored.'

'I wish it wasn't your second honeymoon. Was the first very exciting – in Paris?'

'We could only afford a week-end,' I said guardedly.

'Did you love her a terrible lot?'

'Listen,' I said, 'it was more than fifteen years ago. You hadn't started school. I couldn't have waited all that time for you.'

'But did you?'

'The night after she left me I took Ramage out to

dinner and stood him the best champagne I could get. Then I went home and slept for nine hours right across the bed. She was one of those people who kick at night and then say you are taking up too much room.'

'Perhaps I'll kick.'

'That would feel quite different. I hope you'll kick. Then I'll know you are there. Do you realize the terrible amount of time we'll waste asleep, not knowing a thing? A quarter of our life.'

It took her a long time to calculate that. She wasn't good at figures as I was. 'More,' she said, 'much more. I like ten hours.'

'That's even worse,' I said. 'And eight hours at the office without you. And food – this awful business of having meals.'

'I'll try to kick,' she said.

That was at lunch-time the day when our so-called luck started. We used to meet as often as we could for a snack at the Volunteer which was just round the corner from my office -- Cary drank cider and had an unquenchable appetite for cold sausages. I've seen her eat five and then finish off with a hard-boiled egg.

'If we were rich,' I said, 'you wouldn't have to waste time cooking.'

'But think how much more time we'd waste eating. These sausages – look, I'm through already. We shouldn't even have finished the caviare.'

'And then the *sole meunière*,' I said.

11

'A little fried spring chicken with new peas.'

'A *soufflé Rothschild*.'

'Oh, don't be rich, please,' she said. 'We mightn't like each other if we were rich. Like me growing fat and my hair falling out...'

'That wouldn't make any difference.'

'Oh yes, it would,' she said. 'You know it would,' and the talk suddenly faded out. She was not too young to be wise, but she was too young to know that wisdom shouldn't be spoken aloud when you are happy.

I went back to the huge office block with its glass, glass, glass, and its dazzling marble floor and its pieces of modern carving in alcoves and niches like statues in a Catholic church. I was the assistant accountant (an ageing assistant accountant) and the very vastness of the place made promotion seem next to impossible. To be raised from the ground floor I would have to be a piece of sculpture myself.

In little uncomfortable offices in the city people die and people move on: old gentlemen look up from steel boxes and take a Dickensian interest in younger men. Here, in the great operational room with the computers ticking and the tape machines clicking and the soundless typewriters padding, you felt there was no chance for a man who hadn't passed staff college. I hadn't time to sit down before a loud-speaker said, 'Mr Bertram wanted in Room 10.' (That was me.)

'Who lives in Room 10?' I asked.

Nobody knew. Somebody said, 'It must be on the eighth floor.' (He spoke with awe as though he were referring to the peak of Everest – the eighth floor was as far as the London County Council regulations in those days allowed us to build towards Heaven.)

'Who lives in Room 10?' I asked the liftman again.

'Don't you know?' he said sourly. 'How long have you been here?'

'Five years.'

We began to mount. He said, 'You ought to know who lives in Room 10.'

'But I don't.'

'Five years and you don't know that.'

'Be a good chap and tell me.'

'Here you are. Eighth floor, turn left.' As I got out, he said gloomily, 'Not know Room 10!' He relented as he shut the gates. 'Who do you think? The Gom, of course.'

Then I began to walk very slowly indeed.

I have no belief in luck. I am not superstitious, but it is impossible, when you have reached forty and are conspicuously unsuccessful, not sometimes to half-believe in a malign providence. I had never met the Gom: I had only seen him twice; there was no reason so far as I could tell why I should ever see him again. He was elderly; he would die first, I would contribute grudgingly to a memorial. But to be summoned from the ground floor to the eighth shook me. I wondered what terrible mistake could justify a reprimand in Room 10; it seemed to be quite possible that our wedding now would never take place at St Luke's, nor our fortnight at Bournemouth. In a way I was right.

3

THE Gom was called the Gom by those who disliked him and by all those too far removed from him for any feeling at all. He was like the weather – unpredictable. When a new tape machine was installed, or new computers replaced the old reliable familiar ones, you said, 'The Gom, I suppose,' before settling down to learn the latest toy. At Christmas little typewritten notes came round, addressed personally to each member of the staff (it must have given the typing pool a day's work, but the signature below the seasonal greeting, Herbert Dreuther, was rubber stamped). I was always a little surprised that the letter was not signed Gom. At that season of bonuses and cigars, unpredictable in amount, you sometimes heard him called by his full name, the Grand Old Man.

And there was something grand about him with his mane of white hair, his musician's head. Where other men collected pictures to escape death duties, he collected for pleasure. For a month at a time he would disappear in his yacht with a cargo of writers and actresses and oddments – a hypnotist, a man who had invented a new rose or discovered something about the endocrine glands. We on the ground floor, of course, would never have missed him: we should have known nothing about it if we had not read an account in the papers – the cheaper Sunday papers followed the progress of the yacht from port to port: they associated yachts with scandal, but there would never be any scandal on Dreuther's boat. He hated unpleasantness outside office hours.

I knew a little more than most from my position: diesel oil was included with wine under the general heading of Entertainment. At one time that caused trouble with Sir Walter Blixon. My chief told me about it. Blixon was the other power at No. 45. He held about as many shares as Dreuther, but he was not proportionally consulted. He was small, spotty, undistinguished, and consumed with jealousy. He could have had a yacht himself, but nobody would have sailed with him. When he objected to the diesel oil, Dreuther magnanimously gave way and then proceeded to knock all private petrol from the firm's account. As he lived in London he employed the firm's car, but Blixon had a house in Hampshire. What Dreuther courteously called a compromise was reached – things were to remain as they were. When Blixon managed somehow to procure himself a knighthood, he gained a momentary advantage until the rumour was said to have reached him that Dreuther had refused one in the same Honours List. One thing was certainly true – at a dinner party to which Blixon and my chief had been invited, Dreuther was heard to oppose a knighthood for a certain artist. 'Impossible. He couldn't accept it. An

O.M. (or possibly a C.H.) are the only honours that remain respectable.' It made matters worse that Blixon had never heard of the C.H.

But Blixon bided his time. One more packet of shares would give him control and we used to believe that his chief prayer at night (he was a churchwarden in Hampshire) was that these shares would reach the market while Dreuther was at sea.

4

WITH despair in my heart I knocked on the door of No. 10 and entered, but even in my despair I memorized details – they would want to know them on the ground floor. The room was not like an office at all – there was a bookcase containing sets of English classics and it showed Dreuther's astuteness that Trollope was there and not Dickens, Stevenson and not Scott, thus giving an appearance of personal taste. There was an unimportant Renoir and a lovely little Boudin on the far wall, and one noticed at once that there was a sofa but not a desk. The few visible files were stacked on a Regency table, and Blixon and my chief and a stranger sat uncomfortably on the edge of easy chairs. Dreuther was almost out of sight – he lay practically on his spine in the largest and deepest chair, holding some papers above his head and scowling at them through the thickest glasses I have ever seen on a human face.

'It is fantastic and it cannot be true,' he was saying in his deep guttural voice.

'I don't see the importance . . .' Blixon said.

Dreuther took off his glasses and gazed across the room at me. 'Who are you?' he asked.

'This is Mr Bertram, my assistant,' the chief accountant said.

'What is he doing here?'

'You told me to send for him.'

'I remember,' Dreuther said. 'But that was half an hour ago.'

'I was out at lunch, sir.'

'Lunch?' Dreuther asked as though it were a new word.

'It was during the lunch hour, Mr Dreuther,' the chief accountant said.

'And they go out for lunch?'

'Yes, Mr Dreuther.'

'All of them?'

'Most of them, I think.'

'How very interesting. I did not know. Do you go out to lunch, Sir Walter?'

'Of course I do, Dreuther. Now, for goodness sake, can't we leave this in the hands of Mr Arnold and Mr Bertram? The whole discrepancy only amounts to seven pounds fifteen and fourpence. I'm hungry, Dreuther.'

'It's not the amount that matters, Sir Walter. You and I are in charge of a great business. We cannot leave our responsibilities to others. The shareholders...'

'You are talking high falutin rubbish, Dreuther. The shareholders are you and I...'

'And the Other, Sir Walter. Surely you never forget the Other. Mr Bertrand, please sit down and look at these accounts. Did they pass through your hands?'

19

With relief I saw that they belonged to a small subsidiary company with which I did not deal. 'I have nothing to do with General Enterprises, sir.'

'Never mind. You may know something about figures – it is obvious that no one else does. Please see if you notice anything wrong.'

The worst was obviously over. Dreuther had exposed an error and he did not really worry about a solution. 'Have a cigar, Sir Walter. You see, you cannot do without me yet.' He lit his own cigar. 'You have found the error, Mr Bertrand?'

'Yes. In the General Purposes account.'

'Exactly. Take your time, Mr Bertrand.'

'If you don't mind, Dreuther, I have a table at the Berkeley...'

'Of course, Sir Walter, if you are so hungry ... I can deal with this matter.'

'Coming, Naismith?' The stranger rose, made a kind of bob at Dreuther and sidled after Blixon.

'And you, Arnold, you have had no lunch?'

'It really doesn't matter, Mr Dreuther.'

'You must pardon me. It had never crossed my mind ... this – lunch hour – you call it?'

'Really it doesn't...'

'Mr Bertrand has had lunch. He and I will worry out this problem between us. Will you tell Miss Bullen that I am ready for my glass of milk? Would you like a glass of milk, Mr Bertrand?'

'No thank you, sir.'

I found myself alone with the Gom. I felt exposed as he watched me fumble with the papers – on the eighth floor, on a mountain top, like one of those Old Testament characters to whom a King commanded, 'Prophesy.'

'Where do you lunch, Mr Bertrand?'

'At the Volunteer.'

'Is that a good restaurant?'

'It's a public house, sir.'

'They serve meals?'

'Snacks.'

'How very interesting.' He fell silent and I began all over again to add, carry, subtract. I was for a time puzzled. Human beings are capable of the most simple errors, the failing to carry a figure on, but we had all the best machines and a machine should be incapable...

'I feel at sea, Mr Bertrand,' Dreuther said.

'I confess, sir, I *am* a little too.'

'Oh, I didn't mean in that way, not in that way at all. There is no hurry. We will put all that right. In our good time. I mean that when Sir Walter leaves my room I have a sense of calm, peace. I think of my yacht.' The cigar smoke blew between us. '*Luxe, calme et volupté,*' he said.

'I can't find any *ordre* or *beauté* in these figures, sir.'

'You read Baudelaire, Mr Bertrand?'

'Yes.'

21

'He is my favourite poet.'

'I prefer Racine, sir. But I expect that is the mathematician in me.'

'Don't depend too much on his classicism. There are moments in Racine, Mr Bertrand, when – the abyss opens.' I was aware of being watched while I started checking all over again. Then came the verdict. 'How very interesting.'

But now at last I was really absorbed. I have never been able to understand the layman's indifference to figures. The veriest fool vaguely appreciates the poetry of the solar system – 'the army of unalterable law' – and yet he cannot see glamour in the stately march of the columns, certain figures moving upwards, crossing over, one digit running the whole length of every column, emerging, like some elaborate drill at Trooping the Colour. I was following one small figure now, dodging in pursuit.

'What computers do General Enterprises use, sir?'

'You must ask Miss Bullen.'

'I'm certain it's the Revolg. We gave them up five years ago. In old age they have a tendency to slip, but only when the 2 and the 7 are in relationship, and then not always, and then only in subtraction not addition. Now, here, sir, if you'll look, the combination happens four times, but only once has the slip occurred . . .'

'Please don't explain to me, Mr Bertrand. It would be useless.'

'There's nothing wrong except mechanically. Put these figures through one of our new machines. And scrap the Revolg (they've served long enough).'

I sat back on the sofa with a gasp of triumph. I felt the equal of any man. It had really been a very neat piece of detection. So simple when you knew, but everyone before me had accepted the perfection of the machine and no machine is perfect; in every join, rivet, screw lies original sin. I tried to explain that to Dreuther, but I was out of breath.

'How very interesting, Mr Bertrand. I'm glad we have solved the problem while Sir Walter is satisfying his carnal desires. Are you sure you won't have a glass of milk?'

'No thank you, sir. I must be getting back to the ground floor.'

'No hurry. You look tired, Mr Bertrand. When did you last have a holiday?'

'My annual leave's just coming round, sir. As a matter of fact I'm taking the opportunity to get married.'

'Really. How interesting. Have you received your clock?'

'Clock?'

'I believe they always give a clock here. The first time, Mr Bertrand?'

'Well ... the second.'

'Ah, the second stands much more chance.'

The Gom had certainly a way with him. He made you talk, confide, he gave an effect of being really

23

interested – and I think he always was, for a moment. He was a prisoner in his room, and small facts of the outer world came to him with the shock of novelty; he entertained them as an imprisoned man entertains a mouse or treasures a leaf blown through the bars. I said, 'We are going to Bournemouth for our honeymoon.'

'Ah, that I do not think is a good idea. That is *too* classical. You should take the young woman to the south – the bay of Rio de Janeiro...'

'I'm afraid I couldn't afford it, sir.'

'The sun would do you good, Mr Bertrand. You are pale. Some would suggest South Africa, but that is no better than Bournemouth.'

'I'm afraid that anyway...'

'I have it, Mr Bertrand. You and your beautiful young wife will come on my yacht. All my guests leave me at Nice and Monte Carlo. I will pick you up then on the 30th. We will sail down the coast of Italy, the Bay of Naples, Capri, Ischia.'

'I'm afraid, sir, it's a bit difficult. I'm very, very grateful, but you see we are getting married on the 30th.'

'Where?'

'St Luke's, Maida Hill.'

'St Luke's! You are being too classical again, my friend. We must not be too classical with a beautiful young wife. I assume she is young, Mr Bertrand?'

'Yes.'

'And beautiful?'

'I think so, sir.'

'Then you must be married at Monte Carlo. Before the mayor. With myself as witness. On the 30th. At night we sail for Portofino. That is better than St Luke's or Bournemouth.'

'But surely, sir, there would be legal difficulties...'

But he had already rung for Miss Bullen. I think he would have made a great actor; he already saw himself in the part of a Haroun who could raise a man from obscurity and make him the ruler over provinces. I have an idea too that he thought it would make Blixon jealous. It was the same attitude which he had taken to the knighthood. Blixon was probably planning to procure the Prime Minister to dinner. This would show how little Dreuther valued rank. It would take the salt out of any social success Blixon might have.

Miss Bullen appeared with a second glass of milk. 'Miss Bullen, please arrange with our Nice office to have Mr Bertrand married in Monte Carlo on the 30th at 4 p.m.'

'On the 30th, sir?'

'There may be residence qualifications – they must settle those. They can include him on their staff for the last six months. They will have to see the British Consul too. You had better speak on the telephone to M. Tissand, but don't bother me about it. I want to hear no more of it. Oh, and tell Sir Walter Blixon that we have found an error in the Revolg machines. They have got to be changed at once. He had better

consult Mr Bertrand who will advise him. I want to
hear no more of that either. The muddle has given
us a most exhausting morning. Well, Mr Bertrand,
until the 30th then. Bring a set of Racine with you.
Leave the rest to Miss Bullen. Everything is settled.'
So he believed, of course, but there was still Cary.

5

THE next day was a Saturday. I met Cary at the Volunteer and walked all the way home with her: it was one of those spring afternoons when you can smell the country in a London street, tree smells and flower smells blew up into Oxford Street from Hyde Park, the Green Park, St James's, Kensington Gardens.

'Oh,' she said, 'I wish we could go a long, long way to somewhere very hot and very gay and very –' I had to pull her back or she would have been under a bus. I was always saving her from buses and taxis – sometimes I wondered how she kept alive when I wasn't there.

'Well,' I said, 'we can,' and while we waited for the traffic lights to change I told her.

I don't know why I expected such serious opposition: perhaps it was partly because she had been so set on a church wedding, the choir and the cake and all the nonsense. 'Think,' I said, 'to be married in Monte Carlo instead of Maida Hill. The sea down below and the yacht waiting ...' As I had never been there, the details rather petered out.

She said, 'There's sea at Bournemouth too. Or so I've heard.'

'The Italian coast.'

'In company with your Mr Dreuther.'

'We won't share a cabin with him,' I said, 'and I don't suppose the hotel in Bournemouth will be quite empty.'

'Darling, I did want to be married at St Luke's.'

'Think of the Town Hall at Monte Carlo – the mayor in all his robes – the, the . . .'

'Does it count?'

'Of course it counts.'

'It would be rather fun if it didn't count, and then we could marry at St Luke's when we came back.'

'That would be living in sin.'

'I'd love to live in sin.'

'You could,' I said, 'any time. This afternoon.'

'Oh, I don't count London,' she said. 'That would be just making love. Living in sin is – oh, striped umbrellas and 80 in the shade and grapes – and a fearfully gay bathing suit. I'll have to have a new bathing suit.'

I thought all was well then, but she caught sight of one of those pointed spires sticking up over the plane trees a square ahead. 'We've sent out all the invitations. What will Aunt Marion say?' (She had lived with Aunt Marion ever since her parents were killed in the blitz.)

'Just tell her the truth. She'd much rather get picture-postcards from Italy than from Bournemouth.'

'It will hurt the Vicar's feelings.'

'Only to the extent of a fiver.'

28

'Nobody will really believe we are married.' She added a moment later (she was nothing if not honest), 'That will be fun.'

Then the pendulum swung again and she went thoughtfully on, 'You are only hiring your clothes. But my dress is being made.'

'There's time to turn it into an evening dress. After all, that's what it would have become anyway.'

The church loomed in sight: it was a hideous church, but no more hideous than St Luke's. It was grey and flinty and soot-stained, with reddish steps to the street the colour of clay and a text on a board that said, 'Come to Me all ye who are heavy laden,' as much as to say, 'Abandon Hope.' A wedding had just taken place, and there was a dingy high-tide line of girls with perambulators and squealing children and dogs and grim middle-aged matrons who looked as though they had come to curse.

I said, 'Let's watch. This might be happening to us.'

A lot of girls in long mauve dresses with lacy Dutch caps came out and lined the steps: they looked with fear at the nursemaids and the matrons and one or two giggled nervously – you could hardly blame them. Two photographers set up cameras to cover the entrance, an arch which seemed to be decorated with stone clover leaves, and then the victims emerged followed by a rabble of relatives.

'It's terrible,' Cary said, 'terrible. To think that might be you and me.'

'Well, you haven't an incipient goitre and I'm – well, damn it, I don't blush and I know where to put my hands.'

A car was waiting decorated with white ribbons and all the bridesmaids produced bags of paper rose petals and flung them at the young couple.

'They are lucky,' I said. 'Rice is still short, but I'm certain Aunt Marion can pull strings with the grocer.'

'She'd never do such a thing.'

'You can trust no one at a wedding. It brings out a strange atavistic cruelty. Now that they are not allowed to bed the bride, they try to damage the bridegroom. Look,' I said, clutching Cary's arm. A small boy, encouraged by one of the sombre matrons, had stolen up to the door of the car and, just as the bridegroom stooped to climb in, he launched at close range a handful of rice full in the unfortunate young man's face.

'When you can only spare a cupful,' I said, 'you are told to wait until you can see the whites of your enemy's eyes.'

'But it's terrible,' Cary said.

'That, my dear child, is what is called a church marriage.'

'But ours wouldn't be like that. It's going to be very quiet – only near relatives.'

'You forget the highways and the hedges. It's a Christian tradition. That boy wasn't a relation. Trust me. I know. I've been married in church myself.'

'You were married in church? You never told me,' she said. 'In that case I'd *much* rather be married in a town hall. You haven't been married in a town hall too, have you?'

'No, it will be the first time – and the last time.'

'Oh, for God's sake,' Cary said, 'touch wood.'

So there she was two weeks later rubbing away at the horse's knee, asking for luck, and the great lounge of the Monte Carlo hotel spread emptily around us, and I said, 'That's that. We're alone, Cary.' (One didn't count the receptionist and the cashier and the concierge and the two men with our luggage and the old couple sitting on a sofa, for Mr Dreuther, they told me, had not yet arrived and we had the night to ourselves.)

6

WE had dinner on the terrace of the hotel and watched people going into the Casino. Cary said, 'We ought to look in for the fun. After all, we aren't gamblers.'

'We couldn't be,' I said, 'not with fifty pounds basic.' We had decided not to use her allowance in case we found ourselves able to go to Le Touquet for a week in the winter.

'You are an accountant,' Cary said. 'You ought to know all about systems.'

'Systems are damned expensive,' I said. I had discovered that we had a suite already booked for us by Miss Bullen and I had no idea what it would cost. Our passports were still under different names, so I suppose it was reasonable that we should have two rooms, but the sitting-room seemed unnecessary. Perhaps we were supposed to entertain in it after the wedding. I said, 'You need a million francs* to play a system, and then you are up against the limit. The bank can't lose.'

'I thought someone broke the bank once.'

'Only in a comic song,' I said.

'It would be awful if we were really gamblers,' she said. 'You've got to care so much about money. You don't, do you?'

* At the period of this story the franc stood at about 1,200 francs to the pound.

'No,' I said and meant it. All I had in my mind that night was the wonder whether we would sleep together. We never had. It was that kind of marriage. I had tried the other kind, and now I would have waited months if I could gain in that way all the rest of the years. But tonight I didn't want to wait any longer. I was as fussed as a young man – I found I could no longer see into Cary's mind. She was twenty years younger, she had never been married before, and the game was all in her hands. I couldn't even interpret what she said to me. For instance as we crossed to the Casino she said, 'We'll only stay ten minutes. I'm terribly tired.' Was that hint in my favour or against me? Or was it just a plain statement of fact? Had the problem in my mind never occurred to her, or had she already made up her mind so certainly that the problem didn't exist? Was she assuming I knew the reason?

I had thought when they showed us our rooms I would discover, but all she had said with enormous glee was, 'Darling. What extravagance.'

I took the credit from Miss Bullen. 'It's only for one night. Then we'll be on the boat.' There was one huge double room and one very small single room and a medium-sized sitting-room in between: all three had balconies. I felt as though we had taken the whole front of the hotel. First she depressed me by saying, 'We could have had two single rooms,' and then she contradicted that by saying, 'All the beds are double ones,' and then down I went again when she looked at the sofa in the sitting-room and said, 'I wouldn't have minded sleeping on that.' I was no wiser, and so we talked about systems. I didn't care a damn for systems.

After we had shown our passports and got our tickets we entered what they call the *cuisine*, where the small stakes are laid. 'This is where I belong,' Cary said, and nothing was less true. The old veterans sat around the tables with their charts and their pads and their pencils, making notes of every number. They looked, some of them, like opium smokers, dehydrated. There was a very tiny brown old lady with a straw hat of forty years ago covered in daisies: her left claw rested on the edge of the table like the handle of an umbrella and her right held a chip worth one hundred francs. After the ball had rolled four times she placed her piece and lost it. Then she began waiting again. A young man leant over her shoulder, staked 100 on the last twelve numbers, won and departed. 'There goes a wise man,' I said, but when we came opposite the bar, he was there with a glass of beer and a sandwich. 'Celebrating three hundred francs,' I said.

'Don't be mean. Watch him, I believe that's the first food he's had today.'

I was on edge with wanting her, and I flared suddenly up; foolishly, for she would never have looked twice at him otherwise. So it is we prepare our own dooms. I said, 'You wouldn't call me mean if he weren't young and good-looking.'

34

'Darling,' she said with astonishment, 'I was only – ' and then her mouth hardened. 'You *are* mean now,' she said. 'I'm damned if I'll apologize.' She stood and stared at the young man until he raised his absurd romantic hungry face and looked back at her. 'Yes,' she said, 'he is young, he is good-looking,' and walked straight out of the Casino. I followed saying, 'Damn, damn, damn,' under my breath. I knew now how we'd spend the night.

We went up in the lift in a dead silence and marched down the corridor and into the sitting-room.

'You can have the large room,' she said.

'No, you can.'

'The small one's quite big enough for me. I don't like huge rooms.'

'Then I'll have to change the luggage. They've put yours in the large room.'

'Oh, all right,' she said and went into it and shut the door without saying good night. I began to get angry with her as well as myself – 'a fine first night of marriage,' I said aloud, kicking my suitcase, and then I remembered we weren't married yet, and everything seemed silly and wasteful.

I put on my dressing-gown and went out on to my balcony. The front of the Casino was floodlit: it looked a cross between a Balkan palace and a super-cinema with the absurd statuary sitting on the edge of the green roof looking down at the big portico and the commissionaires; everything stuck out in the white light as though projected in 3D. In the harbour the yachts were all lit up, and a rocket burst in the air over the hill of Monaco. It was so stupidly romantic I could have wept.

'Fireworks, darling,' a voice said, and there was Cary on her balcony with all the stretch of the sitting-room between us. 'Fireworks,' she said, 'isn't that just our luck?' so I knew all was right again.

'Cary,' I said – we had to raise our voices to carry. 'I'm so sorry ...'

'Do you think there'll be a Catherine-wheel?'

'I wouldn't be surprised.'

'Do you see the lights in the harbour?'

'Yes.'

'Do you think Mr Dreuther's arrived?'

'I expect he'll sail in at the last moment tomorrow.'

'Could we get married without him? I mean he's a witness, isn't he, and his engine might have broken down or he might have been wrecked at sea or there might be a storm or something.'

'I think we could manage without him.'

'You do think it's arranged all right, don't you?'

'Oh yes, Miss Bullen's done it all. Four o'clock tomorrow.'

'I'm getting hoarse, are you, from shouting? Come on to the next balcony, darling.'

I went into the sitting-room and out on to the balcony there. She said, 'I suppose we'll all have to have lunch together – you and me and your Gom?'

'If he gets in for lunch.'

36

'It would be rather fun, wouldn't it, if he were a bit late. I like this hotel.'

'We'd have just enough money for two days, I suppose.'

'We could always run up terrible bills,' she said, and then added, 'not so much fun really as living in sin, I suppose. I wonder if that young man's in debt.'

'I wish you'd forget him.'

'Oh, I'm not a bit interested in him, darling. I don't like young men. I expect I've got a father fixation.'

'Damn it, Cary,' I said, 'I'm not as old as that.'

'Oh yes, you are,' she said, 'puberty begins at fourteen.'

'Then in fifteen years from tonight you may be a grandmother.'

'Tonight?' she said nervously, and then fell silent. The fireworks exploded in the sky. I said. 'There's your Catherine-wheel.'

She turned and looked palely at it.

'What are you thinking, Cary?'

'It's so strange,' she said. 'We are going to be together now for years and years and years. Darling, do you think we'll have enough to talk about?'

'We needn't only talk.'

'Darling, I'm serious. Have we got *anything* in common? I'm terribly bad at mathematics. And I don't understand poetry. You do.'

'You don't need to – you are the poetry.'

'No, but really – I'm serious.'

'We haven't dried up yet, and we've been doing nothing else but talk.'

'It would be so terrible,' she said, 'if we became a couple. You know what I mean. You with your paper. Me with my knitting.'

'You don't know how to knit.'

'Well, playing patience then. Or listening to the radio. Or watching television. We'll never have a television, will we?'

'Never.'

The rockets were dying down: there was a long pause: I looked away from the lights in the harbour. She was squatted on the floor of the balcony, her head against the side, and she was fast asleep. When I leant over I could touch her hair. She woke at once.

'Oh, how silly. I was dozing.'

'It's bed-time.'

'Oh. I'm not a bit tired really.'

'You said you were.'

'It's the fresh air. It's so nice in the fresh air.'

'Then come on my balcony.'

'Yes, I could, couldn't I?' she said dubiously.

'We don't need both balconies.'

'No.'

'Come round.'

'I'll climb over.'

'No. Don't You might . . .'

'Don't argue,' she said, 'I'm here.'

They must have thought us crazy when they came to do the rooms – three beds for two people and not one of them had been slept in.

7

AFTER breakfast we took a taxi to the Mairie – I wanted to be quite certain Miss Bullen had not slipped up, but everything was fixed; the marriage was to be at four sharp. They asked us not to be late as there was another wedding at 4.30.

'Like to go to the Casino?' I asked Cary. 'We could spend, say, 1,000 francs now that everything's arranged.'

'Let's take a look at the port first and see if he's come.' We walked down the steps which reminded me of Montmartre except that everything was so creamy and clean and glittering and new, instead of grey and old and historic. Everywhere you were re-minded of the Casino – the bookshops sold systems in envelopes, '2,500 francs a week guaranteed', the toyshops sold small roulette boards, the tobacconists sold ashtrays in the form of a wheel, and even in the women's shops there were scarves patterned with figures and *manqué* and *pair* and *impair* and *rouge* and *noir*.

There were a dozen yachts in the harbour, and three carried British flags, but not one of them was Dreuther's *Seagull*. 'Wouldn't it be terrible if he'd forgotten?' Cary said.

'Miss Bullen would never let him forget. I expect

he's unloading passengers at Nice. Anyway last night you wanted him to be late.'

'Yes, but this morning it feels scary. Perhaps we oughtn't to play in the Casino – just in case.'

'We'll compromise,' I said. 'Three hundred francs. We can't leave Monaco without playing once.'

We hung around the *cuisine* for quite a while before we played. This was the serious time of day – there were no tourists and the *Salle Privée* was closed and only the veterans sat there. You had a feeling with all of them that their lunch depended on victory. It was long, hard, dull employment for them –a cup of coffee and then to work till lunch-time – if their system was successful and they could afford the lunch. Once Cary laughed – I forget what at, and an old man and an old woman raised their heads from opposite sides of the table and stonily stared. They were offended by our frivolity: this was no game to them. Even if the system worked, what a toil went into earning the 2,500 francs a week. With their pads and their charts they left nothing to chance, and yet over and over again chance nipped in and shovelled away their tokens.

'Darling, let's bet.' She put all her three hundred francs on the number of her age, and crossed her fingers for luck. I was more cautious: I put one *carré* on the same figure, and backed *noir* and *impair* with my other two. We both lost on her age, but I won on my others.

'Have you won a fortune, darling? How terribly clever.'

'I've won two hundred and lost one hundred.'

'Well, buy a cup of coffee. They always say you ought to leave when you win.'

'We haven't really won. We are down four bob.'

'*You've* won.'

Over the coffee I said, 'Do you know, I think I'll buy a system just for fun? I'd like to see just how they persuade themselves ...'

'If anybody could think up a system, it should be you.'

'I can see the possibility if there were no limit to the stakes, but then you'd have to be a millionaire.'

'Darling, you won't really think one up, will you? It's fun pretending to be rich for two days, but it wouldn't be fun if it were true. Look at the guests in the hotel, they are rich. Those women with lifted faces and dyed hair and awful little dogs.' She said again with one of her flashes of disquieting wisdom, 'You seem to get afraid of being old when you're rich.'

'There may be worse fears when you are poor.'

'They are ones we are used to. Darling, let's go and look at the harbour again. It's nearly lunchtime. Perhaps Mr Dreuther's in sight. This place – I don't like it terribly.'

We leant over a belvedere and looked down at the harbour – there wasn't any change there. The sea was very blue and very still and we could hear the voice of a cox out with an eight – it came clearly over the water and up to us. Very far away, beyond the next headland, there was a white boat, smaller than a celluloid toy in a child's bath.

'Do you think that's Mr Dreuther?' Cary asked.

'It might be. I expect it is.'

But it wasn't. When we came back after lunch there was no *Seagull* in the harbour and the boat we had seen was no longer in sight: it was somewhere on the way to Italy. Of course there was no need for anxiety: even if he failed to turn up before night, we could still get married. I said, 'If he's been held up, he'd have telegraphed.'

'Perhaps he's simply forgotten,' Cary said.

'That's impossible,' I said, but my mind told me that nothing was impossible with the Gom.

I said, 'I think I'll tell the hotel we'll keep on one room – just in case.'

'The small room,' Cary said.

The receptionist was a little crass. '*One* room, sir?'

'Yes, one room. The small one.'

'The small one? For you and madame, sir?'

'Yes.' I had to explain. 'We are being married this afternoon.'

'Congratulations, sir.'

'Mr Dreuther was to have been here.'

'We've had no word from Mr Dreuther, sir. He usually lets us know ... We were not expecting him.'

Nor was I now, but I did not tell Cary that. This, after all, Gom or no Gom, was our wedding day. I

43

tried to make her return to the Casino and lose a few hundred, but she said she wanted to walk on the terrace and look at the sea. It was an excuse to keep a watch for the *Seagull*. And of course the *Seagull* never came. That interview had meant nothing, Dreuther's kindness had meant nothing, a whim had flown like a wild bird over the snowy waste of his mind, leaving no track at all. We were forgotten. I said, 'It's time to go to the Mairie.'

'We haven't even a witness,' Cary said.

'They'll find a couple,' I said with a confidence I did not feel.

I thought it would be gay to arrive in a horse-cab and we climbed romantically into a ramshackle vehicle outside the Casino and sat down under the off-white awning. But we'd chosen badly. The horse was all skin and bone and I had forgotten that the road was uphill. An old gentleman with an ear-appliance was being pushed down to the Casino by a middle-aged woman, and she made far better progress down than we made up. As they passed us I could hear her precise English voice. She must have been finishing a story. She said, 'and so they lived unhappily ever after'; the old man chuckled and said, 'Tell me that one again.' I looked at Cary and hoped she hadn't heard but she had. 'Darling,' I said, 'don't be superstitious, not today.'

'There's a lot of sense in superstition. How do you know fate doesn't send us messages – so that we can be prepared. Like a kind of code. I'm always ınventing new ones. For instance' – she thought a moment – 'it will be lucky if a confectioner's comes before a flower shop. Watch your side.'

I did, and of course a flower shop came first. I hoped she hadn't noticed, but 'You can't cheat fate,' she said mournfully.

The cab went slower and slower: it would have been quicker to walk. I looked at my watch: we had only ten minutes to go. I said, 'You ought to have sacrificed a chicken this morning and found what omens there were in the entrails.'

'It's all very well to laugh,' she said. 'Perhaps our horoscopes don't match.'

'You wouldn't like to call the whole thing off, would you? Who knows? We'll be seeing a squinting man next.'

'Is that bad?'

'It's awful.' I said to the cabby, 'Please. A little faster. *Plus vite.*'

Cary clutched my arm. 'Oh,' she said.

'What's the matter?'

'Didn't you see him when he looked round. He's got a squint.'

'But, Cary, I was only joking.'

'That doesn't make any difference. Don't you see? It's what I said, you invent a code and fate uses it.'

I said angrily, 'Well, it doesn't make any difference. We are going to be too late anyway.'

'Too late?' She grabbed my wrist and looked at

my watch. She said, 'Darling, we can't be late. Stop. *Arrêtez*. Pay him off.'

'We can't run uphill,' I said, but she was already out of the cab and signalling wildly to every car that passed. No one took any notice. Fathers of families drove smugly by. Children pressed their noses on the glass and made faces at her. She said, 'It's no use. We've got to run.'

'Why bother? Our marriage was going to be unlucky – you've read the omens, haven't you?'

'I don't care,' she said, 'I'd rather be unlucky with you than lucky with anyone else.' That was the sudden way she had – of dissolving a quarrel, an evil mood, with one clear statement. I took her hand and we began to run. But we would never have made it in time if a furniture-van had not stopped and given us a lift all the way. Has anyone else arrived at their wedding sitting on an old-fashioned brass bedstead? I said, 'From now on brass bedsteads will always be lucky.'

She said, 'There's a brass bedstead in the small room at the hotel.'

We had two minutes to spare when the furniture man helped us out on to the little square at the top of the world. To the south there was nothing higher, I suppose, before the Atlas mountains. The tall houses stuck up like cacti towards the heavy blue sky, and a narrow terracotta street came abruptly to an end at the edge of the great rock of Monaco. A

46

Virgin in pale blue with angels blowing round her like a scarf looked across from the church opposite, and it was warm and windy and very quiet and all the roads of our life had led us to this square.

I think for a moment we were both afraid to go in. Nothing inside could be as good as this, and nothing was. We sat on a wooden bench, and another couple soon sat down beside us, the girl in white, the man in black: I became painfully conscious that I wasn't dressed up. Then a man in a high stiff collar made a great deal of fuss about papers and for a while we thought the marriage wouldn't take place at all: then there was a to-do, because we had turned up without witnesses, before they consented to produce a couple of sad clerks. We were led into a large empty room with a chandelier, and a desk – a notice on the door said *Salle des Mariages*, and the mayor, a very old man who looked like Clemenceau, wearing a blue and red ribbon of office, stood impatiently by while the man in the collar read out our names and our birth-dates. Then the mayor repeated what sounded like a whole code of laws in rapid French and we had to agree to them – apparently they were the clauses from the *Code Napoléon*. After that the mayor made a little speech in very bad English about our duty to society and our responsibility to the State, and at last he shook hands with me and kissed Cary on the cheek, and we went out again past the waiting couple on to the little windy square.

It wasn't an impressive ceremony, there was no organ like at St Luke's and no wedding guests. 'I don't feel I've been married,' Cary said, but then she added, 'It's fun not feeling married.'

8

THERE are so many faces in streets and bars and buses and stores that remind one of Original Sin, so few that carry permanently the sign of Original Innocence. Cary's face was like that – she would always until old age look at the world with the eyes of a child. She was never bored: every day was a new day: even grief was eternal and every joy would last for ever. 'Terrible' was her favourite adjective – it wasn't in her mouth a *cliché* – there *was* terror in her pleasures, her fears, her anxieties, her laughter – the terror of surprise, of seeing something for the first time. Most of us only see resemblances, every situation has been met before, but Cary saw only differences, like a wine-taster who can detect the most elusive flavour.

We went back to the hotel and the *Seagull* hadn't come and Cary met this anxiety quite unprepared as though it were the first time we had felt it. Then we went to the bar and had a drink, and it might have been the first drink we had ever had together. She had an insatiable liking for gin and Dubonnet which I didn't share. I said, 'He won't be in now till to-morrow.'

'Darling, shall we have enough for the bill?'

'Oh, we can manage tonight.'

'We might win enough at the Casino.'

'We'll stick to the cheap room. We can't afford to risk much.'

I think we lost about two thousand francs that night and in the morning and in the afternoon we looked down at the harbour and the *Seagull* wasn't there. 'He *has* forgotten,' Cary said. 'He'd have telegraphed otherwise.' I knew she was right, and I didn't know what to do, and when the next day came I knew even less.

'Darling,' Cary said, 'we'd better go while we can still pay,' but I had secretly asked for the bill (on the excuse that we didn't want to play beyond our resources), and I knew that already we had insufficient. There was nothing to do but wait. I telegraphed to Miss Bullen and she replied that Mr Dreuther was at sea and out of touch. I was reading the telegram out to Cary as the old man with the ear-appliance sat on a chair at the top of the steps, watching the people go by in the late afternoon sun.

He asked suddenly, 'Do you know Dreuther?'

I said, 'Well, Mr Dreuther is my employer.'

'You think he is,' he said sharply. 'You are in Sitra, are you?'

'Yes.'

'Then I'm your employer, young man. Don't you put your faith in Dreuther.'

'You are Mr Bowles?'

'Of course I'm Mr Bowles. Go and find my nurse. It's time we went to the tables.'

When we were alone again, Cary asked, 'Who was that horrible old man? Is he really your employer?'

'In a way. In the firm we call him A. N. Other. He owns a few shares in Sitra – only a few, but they hold the balance between Dreuther and Blixon. As long as he supports Dreuther, Blixon can do nothing, but if Blixon ever managed to buy the shares, I'd be sorry for the Gom. A way of speaking,' I added. 'Nothing could make me sorry for him now.'

'He's only forgetful, darling.'

'Forgetfulness like that only comes when you don't care a damn about other people. None of us has a right to forget anyone. Except ourselves. The Gom never forgets himself. Oh hell, let's go to the Casino.'

'We can't afford to.'

'We are so in debt we may as well.'

That night we didn't bet much: we stood there and watched the veterans. The young man was back in the *cuisine*. I saw him change a thousand francs into tokens of a hundred, and presently when he'd lost those, he went out – no coffee or rolls for him that evening. Cary said, 'Do you think he'll go hungry to bed?'

'We all will,' I said, 'if the *Seagull* doesn't come.'

I watched them playing their systems, losing a little, gaining a little, and I thought it was strange how the belief persisted – that somehow you could beat the bank. They were like theologians, patiently trying to rationalize a mystery. I suppose in all lives a moment comes when we wonder – suppose after all there is a God, suppose the theologians are right. Pascal was a gambler, who staked his money on a divine system. I thought, I am a far better mathematician than any of these – is that why I don't believe in their mystery, and yet if this mystery exists, isn't it possible that I might solve it where they have failed? It was almost like a prayer when I thought: it's not for the sake of money – I don't want a fortune – just a few days with Cary free from anxiety.

Of all the systems round the table there was only one that really worked, and that did not depend on the so-called law of chance. A middle-aged woman with a big bird's nest of false blonde hair and two gold teeth lingered around the most crowded table. If anybody made a *coup* she went up to him and touching his elbow appealed quite brazenly – so long as the croupier was looking elsewhere – for one of his 200-franc chips. Perhaps charity, like a hunched back, is considered lucky. When she received a chip she would change it for two one-hundred-franc tokens, put one in her pocket and stake the other *en plein*. She couldn't lose her hundreds, and one day she stood to gain 3,500 francs. Most nights she must have left the table a thousand francs to the good from what she had in her pocket.

'Did you see her?' Cary asked as we walked to the bar for a cup of coffee – we had given up the gins and Dubonnets. 'Why shouldn't I do that too?'

'We haven't come to that.'

'I've made a decision,' Cary said. 'No more meals at the hotel.'

'Do we starve?'

'We have coffee and rolls at a café instead – or perhaps milk – its more nourishing.'

I said sadly, 'It's not the honeymoon I'd intended. Bournemouth would have been better.'

'Don't fret, darling. Everything will be all right when the *Seagull* comes.'

'I don't believe in the *Seagull* any more.'

'Then what do we do when the fortnight's over?'

'Go to gaol, I should think. Perhaps the prison is run by the Casino and we shall have recreation hours round a roulette wheel.'

'Couldn't you borrow from the Other?'

'Bowles? He's never lent without security in his life. He's sharper than Dreuther and Blixon put together – otherwise they'd have had his shares years ago.'

'But there must be something we can do, darling?'

'Madam, there is.' I looked up from my cooling coffee and saw a small man in frayed and dapper clothes with co-respondent shoes. His nose seemed bigger than the rest of his face: the experience of a lifetime had swollen the veins and bleared the eyes. He carried jauntily under his arm a walking stick that had lost its ferrule, with a duck's head for a handle. He said with blurred courtesy, 'I think I am unpardonably intruding, but you have had ill-success at the tables and I carry with me good tidings, sir and madam.'

'Well,' Cary said, 'we were just going ...' She told me later that his use of a biblical phrase gave her a touch of shivers, of *diablerie* – the devil at his old game of quoting scripture.

'It is better for you to stay, for I have shut in my mind here a perfect system. That system I am prepared to let you have for a mere ten thousand francs.'

'You are asking the earth,' I said. 'We haven't got that much.'

'But you are staying at the Hôtel de Paris. I have seen you.'

'It's a matter of currency,' Cary said quickly. 'You know how it is with the English.'

'One thousand francs.'

'No,' Cary said, 'I'm sorry.'

'I tell you what I'll do,' I said, 'I'll stand you a drink for it.'

'Whisky,' the little man replied sharply. I realized too late that whisky cost 500 francs. He sat down at the table with his stick between his knees so that the duck seemed to be sharing his drink. I said, 'Go on.'

'It is a very small whisky.'

'You won't get another.'

'It is very simple,' the little man said, 'like all great mathematical discoveries. You bet first on one number and when your number wins you stake your gains on the correct transversal of six numbers. The cor-

54

rect transversal on one is 31 to 36; on two 13 to 18; on three ...'

'Why?'

'You can take it that I am right. I have studied very carefully here for many years. For five hundred francs I will sell you a list of all the winning numbers which came up last June.'

'But suppose the number doesn't come up?'

'You wait to start the system until it does.'

'It might take years.'

The little man got up, bowed and said, 'That is why one must have capital. I had too little capital. If instead of five million I had possessed ten million I would not be selling you my system for a glass of whisky.'

He retired with dignity, the ferruleless stick padding on the polished floor, the duck staring back at us as though it wanted to stay.

'I think my system's better,' Cary said. 'If that woman can get away with it, I can ...'

'It's begging. I don't like my wife to beg.'

'I'm only a new wife. And I don't count it begging – it's not money, only tokens.'

'You know there was something that man said which made me think. It's a pure matter of reducing what one loses and increasing what one gains.'

'Yes, darling. But in my system I don't lose anything.'

She was away for nearly half an hour and then

she came back almost at a run. 'Darling, put away your doodles. I want to go home.'

'They aren't doodles. I'm working out an idea.'

'Darling, please come at once or I'm going to cry.'

When we were outside she dragged me up through the gardens, between the floodlit palm trees and the flower-beds like sugar sweets. She said, 'Darling, it was a terrible failure.'

'What happened?'

'I did exactly what that woman did. I waited till someone won a lot of money and then I sort of nudged his elbow and said, "Give." But he didn't give, he said quite sharply, "Go home to your mother," and the croupier looked up. So I went to another table. And the man there just said, "Later. Later. On the terrace." Darling, he thought I was a tart. And when I tried a third time – oh, it was terrible. One of those attendants who light people's cigarettes touched me on my arm and said, "I think Mademoiselle has played enough for tonight." Calling be Mademoiselle made it worse. I wanted to fling my marriage lines in his face, but I'd left them in the bathroom at the hotel.'

'In the bathroom?'

'Yes, in my sponge bag, darling, because for some reason I never lose my sponge bag – I've had it for years and years. But that's not why I want to cry. Darling, please let's sit down on this seat. I can't cry walking about – it's like eating chocolate in the open air. You get so out of breath you can't taste the chocolate.'

'For goodness' sake.' I said, 'If that's not the worst let me know the worst. Do you realize we shall never be able to go into the Casino again – just when I've started on a system, a real system.'

'Oh, it's not as bad as that, darling. The attendant gave me such a nice wink at the door. I know *he* won't mind my going back – but I never want to go back, never.'

'I wish you'd tell me.'

'That nice young man saw it all.'

'What young man?'

'The hungry young man. And when I went out into the hall he followed me and said very sweetly, "Madame, I can only spare a token of one hundred francs, but it is yours." '

'You didn't take it?'

'Yes – I couldn't refuse it. He was so polite, and he was gone before I had time to thank him for it. And I changed it and used the francs in the slot machines at the entrance and I'm sorry I'm howling like this, but I simply can't help it, he was so terribly courteous, and he must be so terribly hungry and he's got a mind above money or he wouldn't have lent me a hundred francs, and when I'd won five hundred I looked for him to give him half and he'd gone.'

'You won five hundred? It'll pay for our coffee and rolls tomorrow.'

'Darling, you are so sordid. Don't you see that for ever after he'll think I was one of those old harpies like Bird's Nest in there?'

'I expect he was only making a pass.'

'You are so sexual. He was doing nothing of the kind. He's much too hungry to make a pass.'

'They say starvation sharpens the passions.'

9

WE still had breakfast at the hotel in order to keep up appearances, but we found ourselves wilting even before the liftman. I have never liked uniforms – they remind me that there are those who command and those who are commanded – and now I was convinced that everybody in uniform knew that we couldn't pay the bill. We always kept our key with us, so that we might never have to go to the desk, and as we had changed all our travellers' cheques on our arrival, we didn't even have to approach the accountant. Cary had found a small bar called the Taxi Bar at the foot of one of the great staircases, and there we invariably ate our invariable lunch and our dinner. It was years before I wanted to eat rolls again and even now I always drink tea instead of coffee. Then, on our third lunch-time, coming out of the bar we ran into the assistant receptionist from the hotel who was passing along the street. He bowed and went by, but I knew that our hour had struck.

We sat in the gardens afterwards in the early evening sun and I worked hard on my system, for I felt as though I were working against time. I said to Cary, 'Give me a thousand francs. I've got to check up.'

'But, darling,' she said, 'do you realize we've only

59

got five thousand left. Soon we shan't have anything even for rolls.'

'Thank God for that. I can't bear the sight of a roll.'

'Then let's change to ices instead. They don't cost any more. And, think, we can change our diet, darling. Coffee ices for lunch, strawberry ices for dinner. Darling, I'm longing for dinner.'

'If my system is finished in time, we'll have steaks ...'

I took the thousand and went into the *cuisine*. Paper in hand I watched the table carefully for a quarter of an hour before betting and then quite quietly and steadily I lost, but when I had no more tokens to play my numbers came up in just the right order. I went out again to Cary. I said, 'The devil was right. It's a question of capital.'

She said sadly, 'You are getting like all the others.'

'What do you mean?'

'You think numbers, you dream numbers. You wake up in the night and say "*Zéro deux*". You write on bits of paper at meals.'

'Do you call them meals?'

'There are four thousand francs in my bag and they've got to last us till the *Seagull* comes. We aren't going to gamble any more. I don't believe in your system. A week ago you said you couldn't beat the bank.'

'I hadn't studied ...'

'That's what the devil said – he'd studied. You'll

be selling your system soon for a glass of whisky.'

She got up and walked back to the hotel and I
didn't follow. I thought, a wife ought to believe in her
husband to the bitter end and we hadn't been married
a week; and then after a while I began to see her
point of view. For the last few days I hadn't been
much company, and what a life it had been – afraid
to meet the porter's eye, and that was exactly what I
met as I came into the hotel.

He blocked my way and said, 'The manager's
compliments, sir, and could you spare him a few
moments. In his room.' I thought: they can't send her
to prison too, only me, and I thought: the Gom, that
egotistical bastard on the eighth floor who has let us
in for all this because he's too great to remember his
promises. He makes the world and then he goes and
rests on the seventh day and his creation can go to pot
that day for all he cares. If only for one moment I
could have had him in my power – if he could have
depended on my remembering *him*, but it was as if
I was doomed to be an idea of his, he would never
be an idea of mine.

'Sit down, Mr Bertram,' the manager said. He
pushed a cigarette box across to me. 'Smoke?' He
had the politeness of a man who has executed many
people in his time.

'Thanks,' I said.

'The weather has not been quite so warm as one
would expect at this time of year.'

'Oh, better than England, you know.'

'I do hope you are enjoying your stay.' This, I supposed, was the routine – just to show there was no ill-feeling – one has one's duty. I wished he would come to an end.

'Very much, thank you.'

'And your wife too?'

'Oh yes. Yes.'

He paused, and I thought: now it comes. He said, 'By the way, Mr Bertram, I think this is your first visit?'

'Yes.'

'We rather pride ourselves here on our cooking. I don't think you will find better food in Europe.'

'I'm sure you're right.'

'I don't want to be intrusive, Mr Bertram, please forgive me if I am, but we have noticed that you don't seem to care for our restaurant, and we are very anxious that you and your wife should be happy here in Monte Carlo. Any complaint you might have – the service, the wine ... ?'

'Oh, I've no complaint. No complaint at all.'

'I didn't think you would have, Mr Bertram. I have great confidence in our service here. I came to the conclusion – you will forgive me if I'm intrusive –'

'Yes. Oh yes.'

'I know that our English clients often have trouble over currency. A little bad luck at the tables can so easily upset their arrangements in these days.'

'Yes. I suppose so.'

'So it occurred to me, Mr Bertram, that perhaps

– how shall I put it – you might be, as it were, a little – you will forgive me, won't you – well, short of funds?'

My mouth felt very dry now that the moment had come. I couldn't find the bold frank words I wanted to use. I said, 'Well,' and goggled across the desk. There was a portrait of the Prince of Monaco on the wall and a huge ornate inkstand on the desk and I could hear the train going by to Italy. It was like a last look at freedom.

The manager said, 'You realize that the Administration of the Casino and of this hotel are most anxious – really most anxious – you realize we are in a very special position here, Mr Bertram, we are not perhaps' – he smiled at his fingernails – 'quite ordinary *hôteliers*. We have had clients here whom we have looked after for – well, thirty years' – he was incredibly slow at delivering his sentence. 'We like to think of them as friends rather than clients. You know here in the Principality we have a great tradition – well, of discretion, Mr Bertram. We don't publish names of our guests. We are the repository of many confidences.'

I couldn't bear the man's rigmarole any more. It had become less like an execution than like the Chinese water-torture. I said, 'We are quite broke – there's a confidence for you.'

He smiled again at his nails. 'That was what I suspected, Mr Bertram, and so I hope you will accept a small loan. For a friend of Mr Dreuther. Mr

Dreuther is a very old client of ours and we should be most distressed if any friend of his failed to enjoy his stay with us.' He stood up, bowed and presented me with an envelope – I felt like a child receiving a good-conduct prize from a bishop. Then he led me to the door and said in a low confidential voice, 'Try our *Château Gruaud Larose* 1934: you will not be disappointed.'

I opened the envelope on the bed and counted the notes. I said, 'He's lent us 250,000 francs.'

'I don't believe it.'

'What it is to be a friend of the Gom. I wish I liked the bastard.'

'How will we ever repay it?'

'The Gom will have to help. He kept us here.'

'We'll spend as little as we can, won't we, darling?'

'But no more coffee and rolls. Tonight we'll have a party – the wedding party.' I didn't care a damn about the *Gruaud Larose* 1934: I hired a car and we drove to a little village in the mountains called Peille. Everything was rocky grey and gorse-yellow in the late sun which flowed out between the cold shoulders of the hills where the shadows waited. Mules stood in the street and the car was too large to reach the inn, and in the inn there was only one long table to seat fifty people. We sat alone at it and watched the darkness come, and they gave us their own red wine which wasn't very good and fat pigeons roasted and fruit and cheese. The villagers laughed in the next room over their drinks, and soon we could hardly see the enormous hump of hills.

'Happy?'

'Yes.'

She said after a while, 'I wish we weren't going back to Monte Carlo. Couldn't we send the car home and stay? We wouldn't mind about toothbrushes tonight, and tomorrow we could go – shopping.' She said the last word with an upward inflexion as though we were at the Ritz and the Rue de la Paix round the corner.

'A toothbrush at Cartier's,' I said.

'Lanvin for two pyjama tops.'

'Soap at Guerlain.'

'A few cheap handkerchiefs in the Rue de Rivoli.' She said, 'I can't think of anything else we'd want, can you? Did you ever come to a place like this with Dirty?' Dirty was the name she always used for my first wife who had been dark and plump and sexy with pekingese eyes.

'Never.'

'I like being somewhere without footprints.'

I looked at my watch. It was nearly ten and there was half an hour's drive back. I said, 'I suppose we'd better go.'

'It's not late.'

'Well, tonight I want to give my system a real chance. If I use 200-franc tokens I've got just enough capital.'

'You aren't going to the Casino?'

'Of course I am.'

'But that's stealing.'

'No it isn't. He gave us the money to enjoy ourselves with.'

'Then half of it's mine. You shan't gamble with my half.'

'Dear, be reasonable. I need the capital. The system needs the capital. When I've won you shall have the whole lot back with interest. We'll pay our bills, we'll come back here if you like for all the rest of our stay.'

'You'll never win. Look at the others.'

'They aren't mathematicians. I am.'

An old man with a beard guided us to our car through the dark arched streets: she wouldn't speak, she wouldn't even take my arm. I said, 'This is our celebration night, darling. Don't be mean.'

'What have I said that's mean?' How they defeat us with their silences: one can't repeat a silence or throw it back as one can a word. In the same silence we drove home. As we came out over Monaco the city was floodlit, the Museum, the Casino, the Cathedral, the Palace – the fireworks went up from the rock. It was the last day of a week of illuminations: I remembered the first day and our quarrel and the three balconies.

I said, 'We've never seen the *Salle Privée*. We must go there tonight.'

'What's special about tonight?' she said.

'*Le mari doit protection à sa femme, la femme obéissance à son mari.*'

'What on earth are you talking about?'

'You told the mayor you agreed to that. There's another article you agreed to – "The wife is obliged to live with her husband and to follow him wherever he judges it right to reside." Well, tonight we are damned well going to reside in the *Salle Privée.*'

'I didn't understand what he was saying.' The worst was always over when she consented to argue.

'Please, dear, come and see my system win.'

'I shall only see it lose,' she said and she spoke with strict accuracy.

At 10.30 exactly I began to play and to lose and I lost steadily. I couldn't change tables because this was the only table in the *Salle Privée* at which one could play with a 200-franc minimum. Cary wanted me to stop when I had lost half of the manager's loan, but I still believed that the moment would come, the tide turn, my figures prove correct.

'How much is left?' she asked.

'This.' I indicated the five two-hundred-franc tokens. She got up and left me: I think she was crying, but I couldn't follow her without losing my place at the table.

And when I came back to our room in the hotel I was crying too – there are occasions when a man can cry without shame. She was awake: I could tell by the way she had dressed herself for bed how coldly she was awaiting me. She never wore the bottoms of

67

her pyjamas except to show anger or indifference, but when she saw me sitting there on the end of the bed, shaking with the effort to control my tears, her anger went. She said, 'Darling, don't take on so. We'll manage somehow.' She scrambled out of bed and put her arms round me. 'Darling,' she said, 'I've been mean to you. It might happen to anybody. Look, we'll try the ices, not the coffee and rolls, and the *Seagull*'s sure to come. Sooner or later.'

'I don't mind now if it never comes,' I said.

'Don't be bitter, darling. It happens to everybody, losing.'

'But I haven't lost,' I said, 'I've won.'

She took her arms away. 'Won?'

'I've won five million francs.'

'Then why are you crying?'

'I'm laughing. We are rich.'

'Oh, you beast,' she said, 'and I was sorry for you,' and she scrambled back under the bedclothes.

PART TWO

1

ONE adapts oneself to money much more easily than to poverty: Rousseau might have written that man was born rich and is everywhere impoverished. It gave me great satisfaction to pay back the manager and leave my key at the desk. I frequently rang the bell for the pleasure of confronting a uniform without shame. I made Cary have an Elizabeth Arden treatment, and I ordered the *Gruaud Larose* 1934 (I even sent it back because it was not the right temperature). I had our things moved to a suite and I hired a car to take us to the beach. At the beach I hired one of the private bungalows where we could sunbathe, cut off by bushes and shrubs from the eyes of common people. There all day I worked in the sun (for I was not yet quite certain of my system) while Cary read (I had even bought her a new book).

I discovered that, as on the stock exchange, money bred money. I would now use ten-thousand-franc squares instead of two-hundred-franc tokens, and inevitably at the end of the day I found myself richer by several million. My good fortune became known: casual players would bet on the squares where I had laid my biggest stake, but they had not protected themselves, as I had with my other stakes, and it was seldom that they won. I noted a strange aspect of human nature, that though my system worked and theirs did not, the veterans never lost faith in their own calculations – not one abandoned his elaborate schemes, which led to nothing but loss, to follow my victorious method. The second day, when I had already increased my five million to nine, I heard an old lady say bitterly, 'What deplorable luck,' as though it were my good fortune alone that prevented the wheel revolving to her system.

On the third day I began to attend the Casino for longer hours – I would put in three hours in the morning in the kitchen and the same in the afternoon, and then of course in the evening I settled down to my serious labour in the *Salle Privée*. Cary had accompanied me on the second day and I had given her a few thousand francs to play with (she invariably lost them), but on the third day I thought it best to ask her to stay away. I found her anxious presence at my elbow distracting, and twice I made a miscalculation because she spoke to me. 'I love you very much, darling,' I said to her, 'but work is work. You go and sunbathe, and we'll see each other for meals.'

'Why do they call it a game of chance?' she said.

'How do you mean?'

'It's not a game. You said it yourself – it's work. You've begun to commute. Breakfast at nine thirty sharp, so as to catch the first table. What a lot of beautiful money you're earning. At what age will you retire?'

'Retire?'

72

'You mustn't be afraid of retirement, darling. We shall see so much more of each other, and we could fit up a little roulette wheel in your study. It will be so nice when you don't have to cross the road in all weathers.'

That night I brought my winnings up to fifteen million francs before dinner, and I felt it called for a celebration. I *had* been neglecting Cary a little – I realized that, so I thought we would have a good dinner and go to the ballet instead of my returning to the tables. I told her that and she seemed pleased. 'Tired businessman relaxes,' she said.

'As a matter of fact I am a little tired.' Those who have not played roulette seriously little know how fatiguing it can be. If I had worked less hard during the afternoon I wouldn't have lost my temper with the waiter in the bar. I had ordered two very dry Martinis and he brought them to us quite drowned in Vermouth – I could tell at once from the colour without tasting. To make matters worse he tried to explain away the colour by saying he had used Booth's gin. 'But you know perfectly well that I only take Gordon's,' I said, and sent them back. He brought me two more and he had put lemon peel in them. I said, 'For God's sake how long does one have to be a customer in this bar before you begin to learn one's taste?'

'I'm sorry, sir. I only came yesterday.'

I could see Cary's mouth tighten. I was in the wrong, of course, but I had spent a very long day at the Casino, and she might ha/e realized that I am not the kind of man who is usually crotchety with servants. She said, 'Who would think that a week ago we didn't even dare to speak to a waiter in case he gave us a bill?'

When we went in to dinner there was a little trouble about our table on the terrace: we were earlier than usual, but as I said to Cary we had been good customers and they could have taken some small trouble to please. However, this time I was careful not to let my irritation show more than very slightly – I was determined that this dinner should be one to remember.

Cary as a rule likes to have her mind made up for her, so I took the menu and began to order. 'Caviare,' I said.

'For one,' Cary said.

'What will you have? Smoked salmon?'

'You order yours,' Cary said.

I ordered '*bresse à l'estragon à la broche*', a little Roquefort, and some wild strawberries. This, I thought, was a moment too for the *Gruaud Larose* '34 (they would have learned their lesson about the temperature). I leant back feeling pleased and contented: my dispute with the waiter was quite forgotten, and I knew that I had behaved politely and with moderation when I found that our table was occupied.

'And Madame?' the waiter asked.

'A roll and butter and a cup of coffee,' Cary said.

'But Madame perhaps would like...' She gave him her sweetest smile as though to show me what I had missed. She said, 'Just a roll and butter please. I'm not hungry. To keep Monsieur company.'

I said angrily, 'In *that* case I'll cancel...' but the waiter had already gone. I said, 'How dare you?'

'What's the matter, darling?'

'You know very well what's the matter. You let me order...'

'But truly I'm not hungry, darling. I just wanted to be sentimental, that's all. A roll and butter reminds me of the days when we weren't rich. Don't you remember that little café at the foot of the steps?'

'You are laughing at me.'

'But *no*, darling. Don't you like thinking of those days at all?'

'Those days, those days — why don't you talk about last week and how you were afraid to send anything to the laundry and we couldn't afford the English papers and you couldn't read the French ones and...'

'Don't you remember how reckless you were when you gave five francs to a beggar? Oh, that reminds me...'

'What of?'

'I never meet the hungry young man now.'

'I don't suppose he goes sunbathing.'

My caviare came and my vodka. The waiter said, 'Would Madame like her coffee now?'

'No. No, I think I'll toy with it while Monsieur has his – his ...'

'*Bresse à l'estragon*, Madame.'

I've never enjoyed caviare less. She watched every helping I took, her chin in her hand, leaning forward in what I suppose she meant to be a devoted and wifely way. The toast crackled in the silence, but I was determined not to be beaten. I ate the next course grimly to an end and pretended not to notice how she spaced out her roll – she couldn't have been enjoying her meal much either. She said to the waiter, 'I'll have another cup of coffee to keep my husband company with his strawberries. Wouldn't you like a half bottle of champagne, darling?'

'No. If I drink any more I might lose my self-control ...'

'Darling, what have I said? Don't you like me to remember the days when we were poor and happy? After all, if I had married you now it might have been for your money. You know you were terribly nice when you gave me five hundred francs to gamble with. You watched the wheel so seriously.'

'Aren't I serious now?'

'You don't watch the wheel any longer. You watch your paper and your figures. Darling, we are on *holiday*.'

'We would have been if Dreuther had come.'

'We can afford to go by ourselves now. Let's take a plane tomorrow – anywhere.'

'Not tomorrow. You see, according to my calculations the cycle of loss comes up tomorrow. Of course I'll only use 1,000-franc tokens, so as to reduce the incident.'

'Then the day after . . .'

'That's when I have to win back on double stakes. If you've finished your coffee it's time for the ballet.'

'I've got a headache. I don't want to go.'

'Of course you've got a headache eating nothing but rolls.'

'I ate nothing but rolls for three days and I never had a headache.' She got up from the table and said slowly, 'But in those days I was in love.' I refused to quarrel and I went to the ballet alone.

I can't remember which ballet it was – I don't know that I could have remembered even the same night. My mind was occupied. I had to lose next day if I were to win the day after, otherwise my system was at fault. My whole stupendous run would prove to have been luck only – the kind of luck that presumably by the laws of chance turns up in so many centuries, just as those long-lived laborious monkeys who are set at typewriters eventually in the course of centuries produce the works of Shakespeare. The ballerina to me was hardly a woman so much as a ball spinning on the wheel: when she finished her final movement and came before the curtain alone it was as though she had come to rest triumphantly at zero and all the counters around her were shovelled away into the back – the two thousand francs from the cheap seats with the square tokens from the stalls, all jumbled together. I took a turn on the terrace to clear my head: this was where we had stood the first night watching together for the *Seagull*. I wished Cary had been with me and I nearly returned straight away to the hotel to give her all she asked. She was right: system or chance, who cared? We could catch a plane, extend our holiday: I had enough now to buy a partnership in some safe modest business without walls of glass and modern sculpture and a Gom on the eighth floor, and yet – it was like leaving a woman one loved untouched, untasted, to go away and never know the truth of how the ball had come to rest in that particular order – the poetry of absolute chance or the determination of a closed system? I would be grateful for the poetry, but what pride I should feel if I proved the determinism.

The regiment was all assembled: strolling by the tables I felt like a commanding officer inspecting his unit. I would have liked to reprove the old lady for wearing the artificial daisies askew on her hat and to speak sharply to Mr Bowles for a lack of polish on his ear-appliance. A touch on my elbow and I handed out my 200 token to the lady who cadged. 'Move more smartly to it,' I wanted to say to her, 'the arm should be extended at full length and not bent at the elbow, and it's time you did something about your hair.' They watched me pass with expressions of nervous regret, waiting for me to choose my table, and when I halted somebody rose and offered me a seat. But I had not come to win – I had come symbolically to make my first loss and go. So courteously I declined the seat, laid out a pattern of tokens and with a sense of triumph saw them shovelled away. Then I went back to the hotel.

Cary wasn't there, and I was disappointed. I wanted to explain to her the importance of that symbolic loss, and instead I could only undress and climb between the humdrum sheets. I slept fitfully. I had grown used to Cary's company, and I put on the light at one to see the time, and I was still alone. At half past two Cary woke me as she felt her way to bed in the dark.

'Where've you been?' I asked.

'Walking,' she said.

'All by yourself?'

'No.' The space between the beds filled with her hostility, but I knew better than to strike the first blow – she was waiting for that advantage. I pretended to roll over and settle for sleep. After a long time she said, 'We walked down to the Sea Club.'

'It's closed.'

'We found a way in – it was very big and eerie in the dark with all the chairs stacked.'

'Quite an adventure. What did you do for light?'

'Oh, there was bright moonlight. Philippe told me all about his life.'

'I hope you unstacked a chair.'

'We sat on the floor.'

'If it was a madly interesting life tell it me. Otherwise it's late and I have to be . . .'

79

'"Up early for the Casino." I don't suppose you'd find it an interesting life. It was so simple, idyllic. And he told it with such intensity. He went to school at a *lycée*.'

'Most people do in France.'

'His parents died and he lived with his grandmother.'

'What about his grandfather?'

'He was dead too.'

'Senile mortality is very high in France.'

'He did military service for two years.'

I said, 'It certainly seems a life of striking originality.'

'You can sneer and sneer,' she said.

'But, dear, I've said nothing.'

'Of course you wouldn't be interested. You are never interested in anybody different from yourself, and he's young and very poor. He feeds on coffee and rolls.'

'Poor fellow,' I said with genuine sympathy.

'You are so uninterested you don't even ask his name.'

'You said it was Philippe.'

'Philippe who?' she asked triumphantly.

'Dupont,' I said.

'It isn't. It's Chantier.'

'Ah well, I mixed him up with Dupont.'

'Who's Dupont?'

'Perhaps they look alike.'

'I said who's Dupont.'

'I've no idea,' I said. 'But it's awfully late.'

'You're unbearable.' She slapped her pillow as though it were my face. There was a pause of several minutes and then she said bitterly, 'You haven't even asked whether I slept with him.'

'I'm sorry. Did you?'

'No. But he asked me to spend the night with him.'

'On the stacked chairs?'

'I'm having dinner with him tomorrow night.'

She was beginning to get me in the mood she wanted. I could stop myself no longer. I said, 'Who the hell is this Philippe Chantier?'

'The hungry young man, of course.'

'Are you going to dine on coffee and rolls?'

'I'm paying for the dinner. He's very proud, but I insisted. He's taking me somewhere very cheap and quiet and simple – a sort of students' place.'

'That's lucky,' I said, 'because I'm dining out too. Someone I met tonight at the Casino.'

'Who?'

'A Madame Dupont.'

'There's no such name.'

'I couldn't tell you the right one. I'm careful of a woman's honour.'

'Who is she?'

'She was winning a lot tonight at baccarat and we got into conversation. Her husband died recently, she was very fond of him, and she's sort of drowning her sorrows. I expect she'll soon find comfort, because she's young and beautiful and intelligent and rich.'

'Where are you having dinner?'

'Well, I don't want to bring her here – there might be talk. And she's too well known at the *Salle Privée*. She suggested driving to Cannes where nobody would know us.'

'Well, don't bother to come back early. I shall be late.'

'Exactly what I was going to say to you, dear.'

It was that sort of night. As I lay awake – and was aware of her wakefulness a few feet away – I thought it's the Gom's doing, he's even ruining our marriage now. I said, 'Dear, if you'll give up your dinner, I'll give up mine.'

She said, 'I don't even believe in yours. You invented it.'

'I swear to you – word of honour – that I'm giving a woman dinner tomorrow night.'

She said, 'I can't let Philippe down.' I thought gloomily: now I've got to do it, and where the hell can I find a woman?

2

WE were very polite to each other at breakfast and at lunch. Cary even came into the Casino with me in the early evening, but I think her sole motive was to spot my woman. As it happened a young woman of great beauty was sitting at one of the tables, and Cary obviously drew the incorrect conclusion. She tried to see whether we exchanged glances and at last she could restrain her curiosity no longer. She said to me, 'Aren't you going to speak to her?'

'Who?'

'That girl.'

'I don't know what you mean,' I said, and tried to convey in my tone of voice that I was still guarding the honour of another. Cary said furiously, 'I must be off. I can't keep Philippe waiting. He's so sensitive.'

My system was working: I was losing exactly what I had anticipated losing, but all the exhilaration had gone out of my calculations. I thought: suppose this isn't what they call a lovers' quarrel; suppose she's really interested in this man; suppose this is the end. What do I do? What's left for me? Fifteen thousand pounds was an inadequate answer.

I was not the only one who was losing regularly.

Mr Bowles sat in his wheeled chair, directing his nurse who put the tokens on the cloth for him, leaning over his shoulder, pushing with her private rake. He too had a system, but I suspected that his system was not working out. He sent her back twice to the desk for more money, and the second time I saw that his pocket-book was empty except for a few thousand-franc notes. He rapped out his directions and she laid out his remaining tokens – a hundred and fifty thousand francs' worth of them – the ball rolled and he lost the lot. Wheeling from the table he caught sight of me. 'You,' he said, 'what's your name?'

'Bertram.'

'I've cashed too little. Don't want to go back to the hotel. Lend me five million.'

'I'm sorry,' I said.

'You know who I am. You know what I'm worth.'

'The hotel...' I began.

'They can't let me have that amount till the banks open. I want it tonight. You've been winning plenty. I've watched you. I'll pay you back before the evening's out.'

'People have been known to lose.'

'I can't hear what you say,' he said, shifting his earpiece.

'I'm sorry, Mr Other,' I said.

'My name's not Other. You know me. I'm A. N. Bowles.'

'We call you A. N. Other in the office. Why don't

you go to the bank here and cash a cheque? There's someone always on duty.'

'I haven't got a French account, young man. Haven't you heard of currency regulations?'

'They don't seem to be troubling either of us much,' I said.

'You'd better come and have a cup of coffee and discuss the matter.'

'I'm busy just now.'

'Young man,' the Other said, 'I'm your employer.'

'I don't recognize anybody but the Gom.'

'Who on earth is the Gom?'

'Mr Dreuther.'

'The Gom. A.N. Other. There seems to be a curious lack of respect for the heads of your firm. Sir Walter Blixon – has he a name?'

'I believe the junior staff know him as the Blister.'

A thin smile momentarily touched the grey powdery features. 'At least that name is expressive,' A. N. Other remarked. 'Nurse, you can take a walk for half an hour. You can go as far as the harbour and back. You've always told me you like boats.'

When I turned the chair and began to push Bowles into the bar, a slight sweat had formed on my forehead and hands. An idea had come to me so fantastic that it drove away the thought of Cary and her hungry squire. I couldn't even wait till I got to the bar. I said, 'I've got fifteen million francs in my safe deposit box at the hotel. You can have them tonight in return for your shares.'

'Don't be a fool. They are worth twenty million at par, and Dreuther or Blixon would give me fifty million for them. A glass of Perrier water, please.'

I got him his water. He said, 'Now fetch me that five million.'

'No.'

'Young man,' he said, 'I have an infallible system. I have promised myself for twenty years to break the bank. I will not be foiled by a mere five million. Go and fetch them. Unless you do I shall order your dismissal.'

'Do you think that threat means anything to a man with fifteen million in the safe? And tomorrow I shall have twenty million.'

'You've been losing all tonight. I've watched you.'

'I had expected to lose. It proves my system's right.'

'There can't be two fallible systems.'

'Yours, I'm afraid, will prove only too fallible.'

'Tell me how yours works.'

'No. But I'll advise you on what is wrong with yours.'

'My system is my own.'

'How much have you won by it?'

'I have not yet begun to win. I am only at the first stage. Tonight I begin to win. Damn you, young man, fetch me that five million.'

'My system has won over fifteen million.'

I had got a false impression that the Other was a calm man. It is easy to appear calm when your movements are so confined. But when his fingers moved an inch on his knee he was exhibiting an uncontrollable emotion: his head swayed a minute degree and set the cord of his ear-appliance flapping. It was like the tiny stir of air clinking a shutter that is yet the sign of a tornado's approach.

He said, 'Suppose we have hit on the same system.'

'We haven't. I've been watching yours. I know it well. You can buy it in a paper packet at the stationer's for a thousand francs.'

'That's false. I thought it out myself, over the years, young man, in this chair. Twenty years of years.'

'It's not only *great* minds that think alike. But the bank will never be broken by a thousand-franc system marked on the envelope Infallible.'

'I'll prove you wrong. I'll make you eat that packet. Fetch me the five million.'

'I've told you my terms.'

Backward and forward and sideways moved the hands in that space to which illness confined him. They ran like mice in a cage – I could imagine them nibbling at the intolerable bars. 'You don't know what you are asking. Don't you realize you'd control the company if you chose to side with Blixon?'

'At least I would know something about the company controlled.'

'Listen. If you let me have the five million tonight, I will repay it in the morning and give you half my winnings.'

'There won't be any winnings with your system.'

'You seem very sure of yours.'

'Yes.'

'I might consider selling the shares for twenty million plus your system.'

'I haven't got twenty million.'

'Listen, if you are so sure of yourself you can take an option on the shares for fifteen million now. You pay the balance in twenty-four hours – 9 p.m. tomorrow – or you forfeit your fifteen million. In addition you give me your system.'

'It's a crazy proposal.'

'This is a crazy place.'

'If I don't win five million tomorrow, I don't have a single share?'

'Not a single share.' The fingers had stopped moving.

I laughed. 'Doesn't it occur to you that I've only got to phone the office tomorrow, and Blixon would advance me the money on the option? He wants the shares.'

'Tomorrow is Sunday and the agreement is for cash.'

'I don't give you my system till the final payment,' I said.

'I shan't want it if you've lost.'

'But I need money to play with.'

He took that carefully in. I said, 'You can't run a system on a few thousand francs.'

'You can pay ten million now,' he said, 'on account of fifteen. If you lose, you'll owe me five million.'

'How would you get it?'

He gave me a malign grin. 'I'll have your wages docked five hundred a year for ten years.'

I believe he meant it. In the world of Dreuther and Blixon he and his small packet of shares had survived only by the hardness, the meanness and the implacability of his character.

'I shall have to win ten million with five million.'

'You said you had the perfect system.'

'I thought I had.'

The old man was bitten by his own gamble: he jeered at me. 'Better just lend me the five million and forget the option.'

I thought of the Gom at sea in his yacht with his headline guests and the two of us forgotten – what did he care about his assistant accountant? I remembered the way he had turned to Miss Bullen and said, 'Arrange for Mr Bertrand (he couldn't bother to get my name right) to be married.' Would he arrange through Miss Bullen for our children to be born and our parents to be buried? I thought, with these shares at Blixon's call I shall have him fixed – he'll be powerless, I'll be employing him for just as long as I want him to feel the sting: then no more room on the eighth floor, no more yacht, no more of his *'luxe, calme et volupté'*. He had taken me in with his culture and his courtesy and his phoney kindness until I had nearly accepted him for the great man he believed himself to be. Now, I thought with a sadness for which I couldn't account, he will be small enough to be in my hands, and I looked at my ink-stained fingers with disrelish.

'You see,' the Other said, 'you don't believe any longer.'

'Oh, yes, I do,' I said, 'I'll take your bet. I was just thinking of something else – that's all.'

3

I WENT and fetched the money and we drew up the option right away on a sheet of notepaper and the nurse – who had returned by then – and the barman witnessed it. The option was to be taken up at 9 p.m. prompt in the same spot next day: the Other didn't want his gambling to be interrupted before his dinner-hour whether by good or bad news. Then I made him buy me a glass of whisky, though Moses had less trouble in extracting his drink from a rock in Sinai, and I watched him being pushed back to the *Salle Privée*. To all intents and purposes, for the next twenty-four hours, I was the owner of Sitra. Neither Dreuther nor Blixon in their endless war could make a move without the consent of their assistant accountant. It was strange to think that neither was aware of how the control of the business had changed – from a friend of Dreuther to an enemy of Dreuther. Blixon would be down in Hampshire reading up tomorrow's lessons, polishing up his pronunciation of the names in Judges – he would feel no exhilaration. And Dreuther – Dreuther was at sea, out of reach, playing bridge probably with his social lions – he would not be touched by the sense of insecurity. I ordered another whisky: I no longer doubted my system and I had no sense of regret. Blixon would be the first to hear: I would telephone to the office on Monday morning. It would be tactful to inform him of the new position through my chief, Arnold. There must be no temporary *rapprochement* between Dreuther and Blixon against the intruder: I would have Arnold explain to Blixon that for the time being he could count on me. Dreuther would not even hear of the matter unless he rang up his office from some port of call. Even that I could prevent: I could tell Arnold that the secret must be kept till Dreuther's return, for then I would have the pleasure of giving him the information in person.

I went out to tell Cary the news, forgetting about our engagements: I wanted to see her face when I told her she was the wife of the man who controlled the company. You've hated my system, I wanted to say to her, and the hours I have spent at the Casino, but there was no vulgar cause – it wasn't money I was after, and I quite forgot that until that evening I had no other motive than money. I began to believe that I had planned this from the first two-hundred-franc bet in the *cuisine*.

But of course there was no Cary to be found – 'Madame went out with a gentleman,' the porter needlessly told me, and I remembered the date at the simple students' café. Well, there had been a time in my life when I had found little difficulty in picking up a woman and I went back to the Casino to fulfil my word. But the beautiful woman had got a man with her now: their fingers nuzzled over their communal tokens, and I soon realized that single women who came to the Casino to gamble were seldom either beautiful or interested in men. The ball and not the bed was the focal point. I thought of Cary's questions and my own lies – and there wasn't a lie she wouldn't see through.

I watched Bird's Nest circling among the tables, making a quick pounce here and there, out of the croupier's eye. She had a masterly technique: when a pile was large enough she would lay her fingers on a single piece and give a tender ogle at the owner as much as to say, 'You are so generous and I am all yours for the taking.' She was so certain of her own appeal that no one had the heart to expose her error. Tonight she was wearing long amber ear-rings and a purple evening dress that exposed her best feature – her shoulders. Her shoulders were magnificent, wide and animal, but then, like a revolving light, her face inevitably came round, the untidy false blonde hair tangled up with the ear-rings (I am sure she thought of her wisps and strands as 'wanton locks'), and that smile fixed like a fossil. Watching her revolve I began to revolve too: I was caught into her orbit, and I became aware that here alone was the answer. I had to dine with a woman and in the whole Casino this was the only woman who would dine with me. As she swerved away from an attendant with a sweep of drapery and a slight clank, clank from her evening bag where I supposed she had stowed her hundred-franc tokens, I touched her hand, 'Dear lady,' I said – the phrase astonished me: it was as though it had been placed on my tongue, and certainly it seemed to belong to the same period as the mauve evening dress, the magnificent shoulders. 'Dear lady,' I repeated with increasing astonishment (I almost expected a small white moustache to burgeon on my upper lip), 'you will I trust excuse a stranger...'

I think she must have gone in constant fear of the attendants because her instinctive ogle expanded with her relief at seeing me into a positive blaze of light: it flapped across the waste of her face like sheet lightning. 'Oh, not a stranger,' she said, and I was relieved to find that she was English and that at least I would not have to talk bad French throughout the evening. 'I have been watching with such admiration your great good fortune.' (She had indeed profited from it on several occasions.)

'I was wondering, dear lady,' (the extraordinary phrase slipped out again) 'if you would do me the honour of dining. I have no one with whom to celebrate my luck.'

'But, of course, colonel, it would be a great pleasure.' At that I really put my hand up to my mouth to see if the moustache were there. We both seemed to have learnt parts in a play – I began to fear what the third act might hold. I noticed she was edging towards the restaurant of the *Salle Privée*, but all my snobbery revolted at dining there with so notorious a figure of fun. I said, 'I thought perhaps – if we could take a little air – it's such a beautiful evening, the heat of these rooms, some small exclusive place...' I would have suggested a private room if I had not feared that my intentions might have been misunderstood and welcomed.

'Nothing would give me greater pleasure, colonel.'

We swept out (there was no other word for it) and I prayed that Cary and her young man were safely at dinner in their cheap café; it would have been intolerable if she had seen me at that moment. The woman imposed unreality. I was persuaded that to the white moustache had now been added a collapsible opera hat and a scarlet lined cloak.

I said, 'A horse-cab, don't you think, on a night so balmy...'

'Barmy, colonel?'

'Spelt with an L,' I explained, but I don't think she understood.

When we were seated in the cab I appealed for her help. 'I am really quite a stranger here. I have dined out so seldom. Where can we go that is quiet ... and exclusive?' I was determined that the place should be exclusive: if it excluded all the world but the two of us, I would be the less embarrassed.

'There is a small new restaurant – a club really, very *comme il faut*. It is called *Orphée*. Rather expensive, I fear, colonel.'

'Expense is no object.' I gave the name to the driver and leant back. As she was sitting bolt upright I was able to shelter behind her bulk. I said, 'When were you last in Cheltenham ... ?'

The devil was about us that night. Whatever I said had been written into my part. She replied promptly, 'Dear Cheltenham ... how did you discover ... ?'

'Well, you know, a handsome woman catches one's eye.'

'You live there too?'

'One of those little houses off Queen's Parade.'

'We must be near neighbours,' and to emphasize our nearness I could feel her massive mauve flank move ever so slightly against me. I was glad that the cab drew up: we hadn't gone more than two hundred yards from the Casino.

'A bit highbrow, what?' I said, glaring up as I felt a colonel should do at the lit mask above the door made out of an enormous hollowed potato. We had to brush our way through shreds of cotton which were meant, I suppose, to represent cobwebs. The little room inside was hung with photographs of authors, actors and film stars, and we had to sign our name in a book, thus apparently becoming life members of the club. I wrote Robert Devereux. I could feel her leaning against my shoulder, squinnying at the signature.

The restaurant was crowded and rather garishly lit by bare globes. There were a lot of mirrors that must have been bought at the sale of some old restaurant, for they advertised ancient specialities like 'Mutton Chopps'.

She said, 'Cocteau was at the opening.'

'Who's he?'

'Oh, colonel,' she said, 'you are laughing at me.'

I said, 'Oh well, you know, in my kind of life one hasn't much time for books,' and suddenly, just under the word Chopps, I saw Cary gazing back at me.

'How I envy a life of action,' my companion said, and laid down her bag – chinkingly – on the table. The whole bird's nest shook and the amber ear-rings swung as she turned to me and said confidingly, 'Tell me, colonel. I love – passionately – to hear men talk of their lives.' (Cary's eyes in the mirror became enormous: her mouth was a little open as though she had been caught in mid-sentence.)

I said, 'Oh well, there's not much to tell.'

'Men are so much more modest than women. If I had deeds of derring-do to my credit I would never tire of telling them. Cheltenham must seem very quiet to you.' I heard a spoon drop at a neighbouring table. I said weakly, 'Oh well, I don't mind quiet. What will you eat?'

'I have such a teeny-weeny appetite, colonel. A *langouste thermidor* . . .'

'And a bottle of the Widow?' I could have bitten my tongue – the hideous words were out before I could stop them. I wanted to turn to Cary and say, 'This isn't me. I didn't write this. It's my part. Blame the author.'

A voice I didn't know said, 'But I adore you. I

adore everything you do, the way you talk, the way you are silent. I wish I could speak English much much better so that I could tell you...' I turned slowly sideways and looked at Cary. I had never, since I kissed her first, seen so complete a blush. Bird's Nest said, 'So young and so romantic, aren't they? I always think the English are too reticent. That's what makes our encounter so strange. Half an hour ago we didn't even know each other, and now here we are with – what did you call it? – a bottle of the Widow. How I love these masculine phrases. Are you married, colonel?'

'Well, in a way ...'

'How do you mean?'

'We're sort of separated.'

'How sad. I'm separated too – by death. Perhaps that's less sad.'

A voice I had begun to detest said, 'Your husband does not deserve you to be faithful. To leave you all night while he gambles...'

'He's not gambling tonight,' Cary said. She added in a strangled voice, 'He's in Cannes having dinner with a young, beautiful, intelligent widow.'

'Don't cry, *chérie*.'

'I'm not crying, Philippe. I'm, I'm, I'm laughing. If he could see me now...'

'He would be wild with jealousy, I hope. Are you jealous?'

'So touching,' Bird's Nest said. 'One can't help listening. One seems to glimpse an entire life...'

The whole affair seemed to me abominably one-sided. 'Women are so gullible,' I said, raising my voice a little. 'My wife started going around with a young man because he looked hungry. Perhaps he was hungry. He would take her to expensive restaurants like this and make her pay. Do you know what they charge for a *langouste thermidor* here? It's so expensive, they don't even put the price on the bill. A simple inexpensive café for students.'

'I don't understand, colonel. Has something upset you?'

'And the wine. Don't you think I had to draw the line at his drinking wine at my expense?'

'You must have been treated shamefully.'

Somebody put down a glass so hard that it broke. The detestable voice said, '*Chérie*, that is good fortune for us. Look – I put some wine behind your ears, on the top of your head ... Do you think your husband will sleep with the beautiful lady in Cannes?'

'Sleep is about all he's capable of doing.'

I got to my feet and shouted at her – I could stand no more. 'How dare you say such things?'

'Philippe,' Cary said, 'let's go.' She put some notes on the table and led him out. He was too surprised to object.

Bird's Nest said, 'They were really going too far, weren't they? Talking like that in public. I love your old-fashioned chivalry, colonel. The young must learn.'

99

She took nearly an hour before she got through her *langouste thermidor* and her strawberry ice. She began to tell me the whole story of her life, beginning over the *langouste* with a childhood in an old rectory in Kent and ending over the ice-cream with her small widow's portion at Cheltenham. She was staying in a little *pension* in Monte Carlo because it was 'select', and I suppose her methods at the Casino very nearly paid for her keep.

I got rid of her at last and went home. I was afraid that Cary wouldn't be there, but she was sitting up in bed reading one of those smart phrase books that are got up like a novel and are terribly bright and gay. When I opened the door she looked up over the book and said, '*Entrez, mon colonel.*'

'What are you reading that for?' I said.

'*J'essaye de faire mon français un peu meilleur.*'

'Why?'

'I might live in France one day.'

'Oh? Who with? The hungry student?'

'Philippe has asked me to marry him.'

'After what his dinner must have cost you tonight, I suppose he had to take an honourable line.'

'I told him there was a temporary impediment.'

'You mean your bad French?'

'I meant you, of course.'

Suddenly she began to cry, burying her head under the phrase book so that I shouldn't see. I sat down on the bed and put my hand on her side: I felt tired: I felt we were very far from the public house at the

100

corner: I felt we had been married a long time and it hadn't worked. I had no idea how to pick up the pieces – I have never been good with my hands.

I said, 'Let's go home.'

'Not wait any more for Mr Dreuther?'

'Why should we? I practically own Mr Dreuther now.'

I hadn't meant to tell her, but out it came, all of it. She emerged from under the phrase book and she stopped crying. I told her that when I had extracted the last fun out of being Dreuther's boss, I would sell my shares at a good profit to Blixon – and that would be the final end of Dreuther. 'We'll be comfortably off,' I said.

'*We* won't.'

'What do you mean?'

'Darling, I'm not hysterical now and I'm not angry. I'm talking really seriously. I didn't marry a well-off man. I married a man I met in the bar of the Volunteer – someone who liked cold sausages and travelled by bus because taxis were too expensive. He hadn't had a very good life. He'd married a bitch who ran away from him. I wanted – oh, enormously – to give him fun. Now suddenly I've woken up in bed with a man who can buy all the fun he wants and his idea of fun is to ruin an old man who was kind to him. What if Dreuther did forget he'd invited you? He meant it at the time. He looked at you and you seemed tired and he liked you – just like that, for no reason, just as I liked you the first time in the Volunteer. That's how human beings work. They don't work on a damned system like your roulette.'

'The system hasn't done so badly for you.'

'Oh yes, it has. It's destroyed me. I've lived for you and now I've lost you.'

'You haven't. I'm here.'

'When I return home and go into the bar of the Volunteer, you won't be there. When I'm waiting at the 19 bus stop you won't be there either. You won't be anywhere where *I* can find you. You'll be driving down to your place in Hampshire like Sir Walter Blixon. Darling, you've been very lucky and you've won a lot of money, but I don't like you any more.'

I sneered back at her, but there wasn't any heart in my sneer, 'You only love the poor, I suppose?'

'Isn't that better than only loving the rich? Darling, I'm going to sleep on the sofa in the sitting-room.' We had a sitting-room again now, and a dressing-room for me, just as at the beginning. I said, 'Don't bother. I've got my own bed.'

I went out on to the balcony. It was like the first night when we had quarrelled, but this time she didn't come out on to her balcony, and we hadn't quarrelled. I wanted to knock on her door and say something, but I didn't know what word to use. All my words seemed to chink like the tokens in Bird's Nests' bag.

4

I DIDN'T see her for breakfast, nor for lunch. I went
into the Casino after lunch and for the first time I
didn't want to win. But the devil was certainly in
my system and win I did. I had the money to pay
Bowles, I owned the shares, and I wished I had lost
my last two hundred francs in the kitchen. After
that I walked along the terrace – sometimes one gets
ideas walking, but I didn't. And then looking down
into the harbour I saw a white boat which hadn't
been there before. She was flying the British flag and
I recognized her from newspaper photographs. She
was the *Seagull*. The Gom had come after all – he
wasn't much more than a week late. I thought, you
bastard, if only you'd troubled to keep your promise,
I wouldn't have lost Cary. I wasn't important enough
for you to remember and now I'm too important for
her to love. Well, if I've lost her, you are going to lose
everything too – Blixon will probably buy your boat.

I walked into the bar and the Gom was there. He
had just ordered himself a Pernod and he was talking
with easy familiarity to the barman, speaking perfect
French. Whatever the man's language he would have
spoken it perfectly – he was of the Pentecostal type.
Yet he wasn't the Dreuther of the eighth floor now –
he had put an old yachting cap on the bar, he had

several days' growth of white beard and he wore an old and baggy pair of blue trousers and a sweat shirt. When I came in he didn't stop talking, but I could see him examining me in the mirror behind the bar. He kept on glancing at me as though I pricked a memory. I realized that he had not only forgotten his invitation, he had even forgotten me.

'Mr Dreuther,' I said.

He turned as slowly as he could; he was obviously trying to remember.

'You don't remember me,' I said.

'Oh, my dear chap, I remember you perfectly. Let me see, the last time we met . . .'

'My name's Bertram.' I could see it didn't mean a thing to him. He said, 'Of course. Of course. Been here long?'

'We arrived about nine days ago. We hoped you'd be in time for our wedding.'

'Wedding?' I could see it all coming back to him and for a moment he was foxed for an explanation.

'My dear chap, I hope everything was all right. We were caught with engine trouble. Out of touch. You know how it can be at sea. Now you are coming on board tonight, I hope. Get your bags packed. I want to sail at midnight. Monte Carlo is too much of a temptation for me. How about you? Been losing money?' He was sweeping his mistake into limbo on a tide of words.

'No, I've gained a little.'

'Hang on to it. It's the only way.' He was rapidly

paying for his Pernod – he wanted to get away from his mistake as quickly as possible. 'Follow me down. We'll eat on board tonight. The three of us. No one else joins the boat until Portofino. Tell them I'll settle the bill.'

'It's not necessary. I can manage.'

'I can't have you out of pocket because I'm late.' He snatched his yachting cap and was gone. I could almost imagine he had a seaman's lurch. He had given me no time to develop my hatred or even to tell him that I didn't know where my wife was. I put the money for Bowles in an envelope and asked the porter to have it waiting for him in the bar of the Casino at nine. Then I went upstairs and began to pack my bags. I had a wild hope that if I could get Cary to sea our whole trouble might be left on shore in the luxury hotel, in the great ornate *Salle Privée*. I would have liked to stake all our troubles *en plein* and to lose them. It was only when I had finished my packing and went into her room that I knew I hadn't a hope. The room was more than empty – it was vacant. It was where somebody had been and wouldn't be again. The dressing-table was waiting for another user – the only thing left was the conventional letter. Women read so many magazines – they know the formulas for parting. I think they have even learned the words by heart from the glossy pages – they are impersonal. 'Darling, I'm off. I couldn't bear to tell you that and what's the use? We don't fit any more.' I thought of nine days ago and how we'd urged the old horse-cab on. Yes, they said at the desk, Madame had checked out an hour ago.

I told them to keep my bags. Dreuther wouldn't want me to stay on board after what I was going to tell him.

5

DREUTHER had shaved and changed his shirt and was reading a book in his little lounge. He again had the grand air of the eighth floor. The bar stood hospitably open and the flowers looked as though they had been newly arranged. I wasn't impressed. I knew about his kindness, but kindness at the skin-deep level can ruin people. Kindness has got to care. I carried a knife in my mind and waited to use it.

'But your wife has not come with you?'

'She'll be following,' I said.

'And your bags?'

'The bags too. Could I have a drink?'

I had no compunction in gaining the Dutch courage for assassination at his own expense. I had two whiskies very quickly. He poured them out himself, got the ice, served me like an equal. And he had no idea that in fact I was his superior.

'You look tired,' he said. 'The holiday has not done you good.'

'I have worries.'

'Did you remember to bring the Racine?'

'Yes.' I was momentarily touched that he had remembered that detail.

'Perhaps after dinner you would read a little. I was once fond of him like you. There is so much that

I have forgotten. Age is a great period of forgetting.'
I remembered what Cary had said – after all, at his
age, hadn't he a right to forget? But when I thought
of Cary I could have cried into my glass.

'We forget a lot of things near at hand, but we remember the past. I am often troubled by the past.
Unnecessary misunderstanding. Unnecessary pain.'

'Could I have another whisky?'

'Of course.' He got up promptly to serve me.
Leaning over his little bar, with his wide patriarchal
back turned to me, he said, 'Do not mind talking. We
are not on the eighth floor now. Two men on holiday.
Friends I hope. Drink. There is no harm, if one is
unhappy, in being a little drunk.'

I was a little drunk – more than a little. I couldn't
keep my voice steady when I said, 'My wife isn't coming. She's left me.'

'A quarrel?'

'Not a real quarrel. Not words you can deny or
forget.'

'Is she in love with someone else?'

'I don't know. Perhaps.'

'Tell me. I can't help. But one needs a listener.'
Using the pronoun 'one' he made mine a general con-
dition from which all men were destined to suffer.
'One' is born, 'one' dies, 'one' loses love. I told him
everything – except what I had come to the boat to
tell him. I told him of our coffee-and-roll lunches, of
my winnings, of the hungry student and the Bird's
Nest. I told him of our words over the waiter, I told

108

him of her simple statement, 'I don't like you any more.' I even (it seems incredible to me now) showed him her letter.

He said, 'I am very sorry. If I had not been – delayed, this would not have happened. On the other hand you would not have won all this money.'

I said, 'Damn the money.'

'That is very easy to say. I have said it so often myself. But here I am –' he waved his hand round the little modest saloon that it took a very rich man to afford. 'If I had meant what I said, I wouldn't be here.'

'I do mean it.'

'Then you have hope.'

'She may be sleeping with him at this moment.'

'That does not destroy hope. So often one has discovered how much one loves by sleeping with another.'

'What shall I do?'

'Have a cigar.'

'I don't like them.'

'You will not mind –' He lit one himself. 'These too cost money. Certainly I do not like money – who could? The coins are badly designed and the paper is unclean. Like newspapers picked up in a public park, but I like cigars, this yacht, hospitality, and I suppose, I am afraid, yes,' he added lowering his cigar-point like a flag, 'power.' I had even forgotten that he no longer had it. 'One has to put up with this money.'

'Do you know where they will be?' he asked me.

'Celebrating, I imagine – on coffee and rolls.'

'I have had four wives. Are you sure you want her back?'

'Yes.'

'It can be very peaceful without them.'

'I'm not looking for peace – yet.'

'My second wife – I was still young then – she left me, and I made the mistake of winning her back. It took me years to lose her again after that. She was a good woman. It is not easy to lose a good woman. If one must marry it is better to marry a bad woman.'

'I did the first time and it wasn't much fun.'

'How interesting.' He took a long pull and watched the smoke drift and dissolve. 'Still, it didn't last. A good woman lasts. Blixon is married to a good woman. She sits next to him in the pew on Sundays, thinking about the menu for dinner. She is an excellent housekeeper and has great taste in interior decoration. Her hands are plump – she says proudly that they are good pastry hands – but that is not what a woman's hands should be for. She is a moral woman and when he leaves her during the week, he feels quite secure. But he has to go back, that is the terrible thing, he has to go back.'

'Cary isn't that good.' I looked at the last of my whisky. 'I wish to hell you could tell me what to do.'

'I am too old and the young would call me cynical. People don't like reality. They don't like common sense. Until age forces it on them. I would say –

bring your bags, forget the whole matter – my whisky supply is large, for a few days anaesthetize yourself. I have some most agreeable guests coming on board tomorrow at Portofino – you will like Celia Charteris very much. At Naples there are several bordels if you find celibacy difficult. I will telephone to the office extending your leave. Be content with adventure. And don't try to domesticate adventure.'

I said, 'I want Cary. That's all. Not adventure.'

'My second wife left me because she said I was too ambitious. She didn't realize that it is only the dying who are free from ambition. And they probably have the ambition to live. Some men disguise their ambition – that's all. I was in a position to help this young man my wife loved. He soon showed his ambition then. There are different types of ambition – that is all, and my wife found she preferred mine. Because it was limitless. They do not feel the infinite as an unworthy rival, but for a man to prefer the desk of an assistant manager – that is an insult.' He looked mournfully at his long cigar-ash. 'All the same one should not meddle.'

'I would do anything . . .'

'Your wife is romantic. This young man's poverty appeals to her. I think I see a plan. Help yourself to another drink while I tell it to you . . .'

PART THREE

1

I WENT down the gang-plank, swaying slightly from
the effect of the whisky, and walked up the hill from
the port. It was a quarter past eight, and the sight of
a clock reminded me for the first time of what I had
not told Dreuther. Dreuther had said, 'Don't use
money. Money is so obviously sordid. But those little
round scarlet disks ... You will see, no gambler can
resist them.' I went to the Casino and looked for the
pair: they were not there. Then I changed all the
spare money I had, and when I came out my pocket
clinked like Bird's Nests' bag.

It took me only a quarter of an hour to find them:
they were in the café where we used to go for our
meals. I watched them for a little, unseen from the
door. Cary didn't look happy. She had gone there,
she told me later, to prove to herself that she no
longer loved me, that no sentiment attached to the
places where we had been together, and she found
that the proof didn't work out. She was miserable to
see a stranger sitting in my chair, and the stranger
had a habit she detested – he stuffed the roll into his
mouth and bit off the buttered end. When he had
finished he counted his resources and then asked
her if she would mind not talking for a minute while
he checked his system. 'We can go up to five hundred

francs tonight in the kitchen,' he said, 'that is five one-hundred-franc stakes.' He was sitting there with a pencil and paper when I arrived.

I said 'Hullo,' from the doorway and Cary turned. She nearly smiled at me from habit – I could see the smile sailing up in her eyes and then she plucked it down like a boy might pluck his kite back to earth, out of the wind.

'What are you doing here?' she said.

'I wanted to make sure you were all right.'

'I am all right.'

'Sometimes one does something and wishes one hadn't.'

'Not me.'

'I wish you'd be quiet,' the young man said. 'What I am working out is very complicated.'

'Philippe, it's – my husband.'

He looked up, 'Oh, good evening,' and began to tap nervously on the table with the end of his pencil.

'I hope you are looking after my wife properly.'

'That's nothing to do with you,' he said.

'There are certain things you ought to know in order to make her happy. She hates skin on hot milk. Look, her saucer's full of scraps. You should attend to that before you pour out. She hates small sharp noises – for instance, the crackle of toast – or that roll you are eating. You must never chew nuts either. I hope you are listening. That noise with the pencil will not please her.'

116

'I wish you would go away,' the young man said.

'I would rather like to talk to my wife alone.'

'I don't want to be alone with you,' Cary said.

'You heard her. Please go.' It was strange how cleverly Dreuther had forecast our dialogue. I began to have hope.

'I'm sorry. I must insist.'

'You've no right . . .'

Cary said, 'Unless you leave us, we'll both walk out of here. Philippe, pay the bill.'

'*Chérie*, I do want to get my system straight.'

'I tell you what I'll do,' I said. 'I'm a much older man than you are, but I'll offer to fight you. If I win, I talk to Cary alone. If you win, I go away and never trouble you again.'

'I won't have you fighting,' Cary said.

'You heard her.'

'Alternatively, I'll pay for half an hour with her.'

'How dare you?' Cary said.

I put my hand in my pocket and pulled out fistfuls of yellow and red tokens – five-hundred-franc tokens, thousand-franc tokens, shooting them out on to the table between the coffee cups. He couldn't keep his eyes off them. They covered his system. I said, 'I'd rather fight. This is all the money I've got left.'

He stared at them. He said, 'I don't want to brawl.'

Cary said, 'Philippe, you wouldn't . . .'

I said, 'It's the only way you can get out of here without fighting.'

'*Chérie*, he only wants half an hour. After all, it's his right. There are things for you to settle together, and with this money I can really prove my system.'

She said to him in a voice to which in the past week I had become accustomed, 'All right. Take his money. Get along into that damned Casino. You've been thinking of nothing else all the evening.'

He had just enough grace to hesitate. 'I'll see you in half an hour, *chérie*.'

I said, 'I promise I'll bring her to the Casino myself. I have something to do there.' Then I called him back from the door, 'You've dropped a piece,' and he came back and felt for it under the table. Watching Cary's face I almost wished I hadn't won.

She was trying hard not to cry. She said, 'I suppose you think you've been very clever.'

'No.'

'You exposed him all right. You've demonstrated your point. What do I do now?'

'Come on board for one night. You've got a separate cabin. We can put you off in Genoa tomorrow.'

'I suppose you hope I'll change my mind?'

'Yes. I hope. It's not a very big hope, but it's better than despair. You see, I love you.'

'Would you promise never to gamble again?'

'Yes.'

'Would you throw away that damned system?'

'Yes.'

There was a song when I was young – 'and then my heart stood still'. That was what I felt when she began to make conditions. 'Have you told him,' she asked, 'about the shares?'

'No.'

'I can't go on that boat with him not knowing. It would be too mean.'

'I promise I'll clear it up – before sleep.'

She had her head lowered, so that I couldn't see her face, and she sat very silent. I had used all my arguments: there was nothing more for me to say either. The night was full of nothing but chinking cups and running water. At last she said, 'What are we waiting for?'

We picked up all the bags and then we walked across to the Casino. She hadn't wanted to come, but I said, 'I promised to bring you.' I left her in the hall and went through to the kitchen – he wasn't there. Then I went to the bar, and then on to the *Salle Privée*. There he was, playing for the first time with a 500-franc minimum. A. N. Other was at the same table – the five-thousand squares littered the table around him. He sat in his chair with his fingers moving like mice. I leant over his shoulder and gave him *his* news, but he made no sign of interest, for the ball was bouncing now around the wheel. It came to rest in zero as I reached Philippe and the bank raked in their winnings.

I said to Philippe, 'Cary's here. I kept my promise.'

'Tell her not to come in. I am winning – except the last round. I do not want to be disturbed.'

'She won't disturb you ever again.'

'I have won 10,000.'

'But it's loser takes all,' I said. 'Lose these for me. It's all I've got left.'

I didn't wait for him to protest – and I don't think he would have protested.

2

THE Gom that night was a perfect host. He showed himself so ignorant of our trouble that we began to forget it ourselves. There were cocktails before dinner and champagne at dinner and I could see that Cary was getting a little uncertain in her choice of words. She went to bed early because she wanted to leave me alone with the Gom. We both came out on to the deck to say good night to her. A small breeze went by, tasting of the sea, and the clouds hid moon and stars and made the riding lights on the yachts shine the brighter.

The Gom said, 'Tomorrow night you shall persuade me that Racine is the greater poet, but tonight let me think of Baudelaire.' He leant on the rail and recited in a low voice, and I wondered to whom it was in the past that the old wise man with limitless ambitions was speaking.

> *Vois sur ces canaux*
> *Dormir ces vaisseaux*
> *Dont l'humeur est vagabonde;*
> *C'est pour assouvir*
> *Ton moindre désir*
> *Qu'ils viennent du bout du monde.'*

He turned and said, 'I am speaking that to you, my

dear, from him,' and he put his arm around her shoulder, and then gave her a push towards the companion-way. She gave a sound like a small animal in pain and was gone.

'What was the matter?' the Gom asked.

'She was remembering something.' I knew what it was she was remembering, but I didn't tell him.

We went back into the saloon and the Gom poured out our drinks. He said, 'I'm glad the trick worked.'

'She may still decide to get off at Genoa.'

'She won't. In any case we'll leave out Genoa.' He added thoughtfully, 'It's not the first time I've kidnapped a woman.'

He gave me my glass. 'I shan't keep you up drinking tonight, but I wanted to tell you something. I'm getting a new assistant accountant.'

'You mean – you are giving me notice?'

'Yes.'

Unpredictable, the old bastard, I thought – to tell me this now, as his guest. Could it be that in my absence he had met and spoken with the Other? He said, 'You'll need a bigger income now you are married. I'm putting Arnold in charge of General Enterprises. You are to be chief accountant in his place. Drink your whisky and go to bed. They are getting up the anchor now.'

When I went down I wondered whether Cary's cabin would be locked, but it wasn't. She sat on one bunk with her knees drawn up to her chin staring through the porthole. The engines had started and we were moving out. The lights of the port wheeled around the wall. She said, 'Have you told him?'

'No.'

'You promised,' she said. 'I can't go sailing down Italy in this boat with him not knowing. He's been so terribly kind ...'

'I owe him everything,' I said. 'It was he who told me how to act to get you back. The trick was his. I could think of nothing. I was in despair.'

'Then you must tell him. Now. At once.'

'There's nothing to tell. You don't think after he'd done that for me, I'd cheat him with Blixon?'

'But the shares?'

'When I went to find Philippe, I took back the money I'd left for the Other. The option's forfeited. The Other's fifteen million richer – and Philippe has our last five million if he hasn't lost it. We are back where we were.' The words were the wrong ones. I said, 'If only we could be.'

'We never can be.'

'Never?'

'I love you so much more. Because I've been terribly mean to you and nearly lost you.'

We said very little for a long time: there was no room for anything but our bodies in the cramped berth, but some time towards morning, when the circle of the porthole was grey, I woke her and told her what the Gom had said to me. 'We shan't be rich,' I added quickly for fear of losing her again, 'but we can afford Bournemouth next year ...'

'No,' she said sleepily. 'Let's go to Le Touquet. They have a Casino there. But don't let's have a system.'

There was a promise I'd forgotten. I got up and took the great system out of my jacket-pocket and tore it in little pieces and threw them through the porthole – the white scraps blew back in our wake.

The sleepy voice said, 'Darling, it's terribly cold. It's snowing.'

'I'll close the porthole.'

'No. Just come back.'

READ MORE IN PENGUIN

In every corner of the world, on every subject under the sun, Penguin represents quality and variety – the very best in publishing today.

For complete information about books available from Penguin – including Puffins, Penguin Classics and Arkana – and how to order them, write to us at the appropriate address below. Please note that for copyright reasons the selection of books varies from country to country.

In the United Kingdom: Please write to *Dept. EP, Penguin Books Ltd, Bath Road, Harmondsworth, West Drayton, Middlesex UB7 ODA*

In the United States: Please write to *Consumer Sales, Penguin Putnam Inc., P.O. Box 999, Dept. 17109, Bergenfield, New Jersey 07621-0120.* VISA and MasterCard holders call 1-800-253-6476 to order Penguin titles

In Canada: Please write to *Penguin Books Canada Ltd, 10 Alcorn Avenue, Suite 300, Toronto, Ontario M4V 3B2*

In Australia: Please write to *Penguin Books Australia Ltd, P.O. Box 257, Ringwood, Victoria 3134*

In New Zealand: Please write to *Penguin Books (NZ) Ltd, Private Bag 102902, North Shore Mail Centre, Auckland 10*

In India: Please write to *Penguin Books India Pvt Ltd, 210 Chiranjiv Tower, 43 Nehru Place, New Delhi 110 019*

In the Netherlands: Please write to *Penguin Books Netherlands bv, Postbus 3507, NL-1001 AH Amsterdam*

In Germany: Please write to *Penguin Books Deutschland GmbH, Metzlerstrasse 26, 60594 Frankfurt am Main*

In Spain: Please write to *Penguin Books S. A., Bravo Murillo 19, 1° B, 28015 Madrid*

In Italy: Please write to *Penguin Italia s.r.l., Via Benedetto Croce 2, 20094 Corsico, Milano*

In France: Please write to *Penguin France, Le Carré Wilson, 62 rue Benjamin Baillaud, 31500 Toulouse*

In Japan: Please write to *Penguin Books Japan Ltd, Kaneko Building, 2-3-25 Koraku, Bunkyo-Ku, Tokyo 112*

In South Africa: Please write to *Penguin Books South Africa (Pty) Ltd, Private Bag X14, Parkview, 2122 Johannesburg*

BY THE SAME AUTHOR

A selection

Brighton Rock

Set in the pre-war Brighton underworld, this is the story of a teenage gangster, Pinkie, and Ida, his personal Fury who relentlessly brings him to justice.

The Power and the Glory

This poignant story set during an anti-clerical purge in one of the southern states of Mexico 'starts in the reader an irresistible emotion of pity and love' – *The Times*

The Comedians

Set in Haiti under a corrupt dictatorship, this is a graphic story about the committed and uncommitted.

The Quiet American

This novel makes a wry comment on European interference in Asia in its story of the Franco-Vietminh war in Vietnam.

The Heart of the Matter

Scobie – a police officer in a West African colony – was a good man, but his struggle to maintain the happiness of two women destroyed him.

The End of the Affair

This frank, intense account of a love-affair and its mystical aftermath takes place in a suburb of war-time London.

Monsignor Quixote

A wonderfully picaresque and profoundly moving tale of innocence at large amidst the shrines and fleshpots of modern Spain.

BY THE SAME AUTHOR

A selection

May We Borrow Your Husband?
and Other Comedies of the Sexual Life

This collection of short stories holds some of Greene's saddest observations on the hilarity of sex.

The Ministry of Fear

'In this his most phantasmagoric study, the story, largely set in the London "blitz", passes through twilit corridors of horror' – *Observer*

A Burnt-Out Case

Philip Toynbee described this novel, set in a leper colony in the Congo, as being 'perhaps the best that he has ever written'.

The Tenth Man

In a prison in Occupied France one in every ten men are to be shot. The prisoners draw lots among themselves – and for rich lawyer Louis Chavel, it seems that his whole life has been leading up to an agonizing and crucial failure of nerve.

and, in one volume

The Third Man

Rollo Martins is invited by his school-friend hero, Harry Lime, to post-war Vienna, 'a smashed dreary city' occupied by four powers . . .

The Fallen Idol

Philip is a small boy left in a large Belgravia house with Baines, the butler, and 'thin, menacing, dusty' Mrs Baines. And Baines has a girl-friend. Soon Philip is 'caught up in other people's darkness' . . .